HEA~~RT~~ ~~PRI~~NCE

BROKEN HEARTS ACADEMY BOOK 1

C.R. JANE

Heartbreak Prince by C. R. Jane

Copyright © 2020 by C. R. Jane

All rights reserved.

No portion of this book may be reproduced in any form or by any electronic or mechanical means, including information storage and retrieval systems, without written permission from the author, except for the use of brief quotations in a book review, and except as permitted by U.S. copyright law.

For permissions contact:

crjaneauthor@gmail.com

This book is a work of fiction. Names, characters, businesses, places, events, locales, and incidents are either the products of the author's imagination or used in a fictitious manner. Any resemblance to actual persons, living or dead, or actual events is purely coincidental.

For all the broken hearted girls...

JOIN C.R. JANE'S READERS' GROUP

Stay up to date with C.R. Jane by joining her Facebook readers' group, C.R.'s Fated Realm. Ask questions, get first looks at new books/series, and have fun with other book lovers!

Join C.R.'s Fated Realm

HEARTBREAK PRINCE

Soulmates. I believe in them. I was lucky enough to have two of them at one point.

The only problem. *My soulmates happened to be twin brothers.*

Caiden was the light to Jackson's dark. And after all that I had been through, the light was what I thought I needed.

When I chose Caiden, I lost Jackson.

Feeling like half a person after Jackson left, I barely survived when tragedy struck and I lost Caiden too.

It took me years to admit to myself that I had chosen wrong from the beginning. I'm ready to admit it to Jackson... only problem, he hates me.
I'm ready to fight for my happily ever after.

But there's a reason they call him the Heartbreak Prince.

HEARTBREAK PRINCE SOUNDTRACK

Why Are You Here
(Machine Gun Kelly)

Chasing Cars
(Snow Patrol)

Yours
(No Love For The Middle Child)

Breathe (2 AM)
(Anna Nalick)

Past Life
(Trevor Daniel)

One Thing Right
(Marshmello & Kane Brown)

Happier
(Marshmello & Bastille)

Kiss Me
(Sixpence None The Richer)

Delicate
(Taylor Swift)

Never Be The Same
(Camilla Cabello)

Without You
(Ingrid Michaelson)

Portions for Foxes
(Rilo Kiley)

I lost my virginity to an angel...but my first and last kiss was with the devil.
And that's everything you need to know about me.

Sometimes when it's really dark outside, and I feel particularly alone. I allow myself to remember us. It doesn't happen often, because I wouldn't be able to function otherwise, but I just wanted you to know that everything about us is like perfect Technicolor in my memory.

1

THEN

I was eight when we met. *Do you remember that?* I was in third grade. I was small for my age, and all the other kids picked on me. They had plenty of things to go after—who my father was, my slight lisp, how my clothes were all too baggy, and how I didn't have a running washing machine at my house, and so oftentimes my clothes weren't quite as clean as they should have been...because washing clothes in the sink could only go so far. All were fair game. My classmates had made my life a living hell all through elementary school. And I expected it to continue...until the two of you started school.

You started a new school that year. You and your brother had just moved into town. You were only a few months older than me, but you weren't scared of anything. And when you saw me on the playground, and you saw how some of the kids had picked up rocks from the ground and were going to throw them at me, you marched right in. And while Caiden was yelling at them to stop, you were the one who actually tackled Marshall, the biggest kid, who had been particularly awful to me for years. And you didn't even know me.

And when you got up after punching him several times, your lip was bleeding, but you gave me the biggest smile and told me it was all going to be okay.

Do you remember that?

Neither of us noticed the fact that Caiden was also looking at me.

Wasn't it funny how a story like ours could happen like that, even at that young of an age?

We were best friends after you and Caiden defended me that day. Maybe the two of you were more than best friends to me, maybe you were my saviors. Because after years of living in hell, you made sure that school became my safe place.

Remember how Caiden always used to bring extra for lunch, and pretend that he wasn't hungry, but he would actually give it to me? I was in the free lunch program, but both of you thought the school lunches were disgusting and wouldn't allow me to eat them. You never noticed how I snuck the cafeteria food in my backpack after I ate what Caiden brought because if I didn't, I wouldn't have had dinner.

Do you remember how you would beg your parents to let me come over? And even though I was dirty and small, and your parents wished you had other friends, you told them that I was yours, and somehow, you got them to listen.

What you didn't know, or you refused to see, was that Caiden also begged your parents just as fiercely, and he also told them that I was his.

I just wanted you to know that if I had known how it all would've ended up, even at eight years old, I would've run as far away from the two of you as I could.

AFTER I TURNED TEN, Dorothy Miller announced to the whole school at lunch that she was going to marry you. So I punched her.

Do you remember that?

For some reason, the cool thing that fall was for everyone to pretend to get married. But you and Caiden were who all the popular girls wanted to marry.

You got jealous because Caiden asked me to marry him first, so you went ahead and pretended to marry Dorothy, even though it made me cry.

Remember showing up at the pretend ceremony during recess? How Caiden stood there looking so serious—well, as serious as an eleven-year-old boy could—and he promised me he was going to love me forever and ever.

You laughed along with the other kids, who laughed because they all knew it was a joke that someone like Caiden would ever really love someone like me.

Remember when you found me crying afterwards, because it was the first time you'd ever laughed at me? Then you started crying because you felt so bad. You told me that even if Caiden loved me, you were going to love me forever and ever, too.

Then you told me you just wanted me to know that you would love me more, no matter what.

And even at ten, I wanted you to kiss me.

When I was twelve, things grew even worse at home. I didn't tell you, because the whole thing was really embarrassing. But you saw bruises on me, and I knew you didn't believe me when I told you I fell down at recess every day playing soccer.

You started walking me home every day after that first time I lied to you. That first day, your parents didn't know where you went, because you hadn't told Caiden, or asked permission. They found us halfway to my house. Your mom was shrieking, because she was so scared. You looked right at her and told her that you had to protect me.

Remember how Caiden got out of the car and hugged me because I was upset that you'd gotten in trouble? Remember how Caiden begged your mom to give me a ride home every day? Remember how she said that she couldn't because she didn't know my mom?

That year was really hard. Maybe all the other years were hard too. But I think what stuck out in my mind about that year was that it was the first time I realized how big the difference between us really was. I had never seen your mom's Range Rover before. I think Mama had sold her car by then to help pay the property taxes on our home.

I told myself in that moment that no matter what, I would keep a small part of myself away from the two of you.

Then you pitched a big fit, and your mom agreed to drop me off that one time, and I realized how hard keeping myself separate from you was going to be.

I was thirteen when Caiden told me you kissed Marcy Thomas. I confronted you and told you that you had ruined everything. I screamed at you about doing it, and you tried to tell me that Marcy was the one that had kissed you. But I didn't care.

We were supposed to be each other's first kiss.

And so when Caiden kissed me under the bleachers a week later...I kissed him back.

It was a fumbling kiss, but still a really good one. And Caiden told me he loved me again, and this time it wasn't because of a fake marriage ceremony. I told him I loved him back, because I did.

But even then, I knew it probably wasn't the same kind of love that he was talking about.

When I got home that night, you don't know this, but I cried. I cried because I wished the whole time that I had been kissing you.

2

NOW

Beeeeeep. Beeeeeep.

The sound of the hospital equipment ground on my nerves more than usual. Why did I do this to myself? Why did I come every week to sit by the bedside of my former boyfriend? Guilt?

After all, it was my fault he ended up here. It was my fault that the world would never see his wide smile, or the dimple that was only on one cheek.

I thought the guilt would fade in time, release itself the way that sorrow and loss often do. But that hadn't been the case. It had been two years, five months, and eighteen days since I last saw his smile. And even then, the aftermath of what happened that night remained emblazoned in my mind, just as vivid as if it happened yesterday.

The memory of his smile had faded though. All I could remember now was the stark grief on his face now when we last spoke.

He should have been taken off the machine years ago, but his parents hadn't been able to do it. One thing was for certain, you couldn't accuse Caiden's parents of neglect. This room was proof of that, more like a shrine than a hospital bed at this point.

I usually came on Fridays, a punishment of sorts, so I would make sure not to be too happy over the weekend. Which really was stupid, because being "too happy" had never been a threat in my life. I was here on a Monday morning, though, today. It marked a special occasion.

Because in just an hour, I would be starting at a new school, and in just an hour, I would see *him*.

Caiden had always known how to handle Jackson. That brand of darkness inside Jackson, unfathomable to so many, had never frightened Caiden. In a way, they were foils of each other. Fraternal twins and the exact opposites. It always caught people off guard though at how sunny Caiden's disposition had always been. With his black as night hair and even darker brown eyes, he stood in sharp contrast to Jackson's sun god looks.

Maybe his Apollo-like aspect was what threw everyone off about Jackson. Going by his looks alone, he should have been happiness and light personified. So when he went black and savagely punched you in the head and knocked you out because you looked at him wrong...you didn't see it coming.

I fiddled with the blanket on Caiden's bed.

"I think I have to stop coming here," I said softly to his prone form.

For a moment, I almost expected him to answer me.

Of course he didn't. He wouldn't answer me ever again.

At least, that was what the doctors thought. His parents still held out hope for a miracle.

"I think it's time for me to move on," I continued. And it was a relief that he couldn't answer back.

Because what people didn't know about Caiden was that underneath his wide smile was a boy who couldn't let me go.

He called me the loveliest kind of pain.

I called him a monster.

3

JACKSON

I woke up from my nightmare sweating, my heart threatening to beat out of my chest as I tried to come down from the terror of my dream. It was always the same. Caiden locked in some kind of dark place, screaming and clawing to get out.

I rubbed my chest, trying to settle the ache tearing a hole inside of me.

The pain and my nightmares had haunted me since Caiden's accident. Even though the doctors told me that it wasn't the case, that he wasn't locked in his mind in a never-ending hell as he tried to wake up...I didn't believe them.

People didn't understand what it was like to be a twin. Caiden had been my best friend since the moment of our creation. Well, my best friend until her, but I didn't think about *her*. Or at least, I didn't admit to thinking about *her*.

Because she was the one responsible for the fact that I would never see Caiden's eyes again, never hear his laugh, and never hear his voice.

I hated Everly James more than I hated anyone else on the face of the Earth.

And the irony of it all was that I used to love her the most of anyone.

EVERLY

I stood staring at the new hell I found myself in. Not that it was meant to be a hell, or that it was a hell to most of the students residing within its walls.

But any place that held Jackson Parker would be hell for me.

Any place that didn't involve him being mine would feel like that.

Rutherford Academy was supposed to be my fresh start. It was a place I didn't belong, but had worked my ass off to get into. Starting junior year of high school, you could attend. The idea was that you would work hard so that you would be able to move into the college portion of the Academy after senior year. Rutherford was considered a cross between the most elite prep school in the country and an Ivy League college rivaling Harvard and Yale in rankings every year.

The people who attended this school would end up running the world. The buildings were named after families like the Vanderbilts and the Rockefellers, but every year, five scholarships were given out to attend the prep school portion of Rutherford. If those five scholarship students did well and were able to maintain an A+ average throughout the eleventh and twelfth grade, they would get a full ride into the college.

And a future filled with possibilities.

While the junior class was kept segregated due to them being underage, the senior classes were housed in the same building where most of the college freshman classes were held.

I had honestly thought twice about accepting the scholarship when I found out. It was doubtful I would be able to go without seeing Jackson. He had started at the school as a junior, right after Caiden's accident. The nickname of Rutherford Academy had soon become Broken Hearts Academy with the way that he took over the school and left ruin and heartbreak among its female population in his wake.

You could start at Rutherford junior year of high school. Even though I'd gotten my acceptance before I'd started sophomore year, letting me know I would be attending there as a junior, it had taken me a while to heal from my injuries from the accident. I'd missed almost all of my sophomore year at my last school. At least I'd been able to complete all my academic work remote. That had been something. It kept my grades up. When junior year came around, I wasn't ready to start at a school like Rutherford, and I'd asked to be allowed to defer until senior year.

Due to the tragic circumstances of my injuries, the Rutherford Dean had agreed, and I had spent my junior year at the public school across town, taking classes and going to rehab. But news of Jackson's exploits still reached me every day. As a junior and then later as a senior in high school, he managed to hang out with seniors in college. They actually listened to him and looked to him as their leader. With Jackson, you soon learned, you were dealing with someone different.

This was my chance though. No one but Jackson and

Caiden had ever believed a girl like me could make something of herself.

If I made it through the next five years, that was a guarantee.

As soon as I walked through the front doors, it was like I'd been transported to a different world. The floors were black marble flecked with gold, and actual chandeliers hung from the ceiling every five feet or so. The front entryway was an enormous rotunda, reminding me of the U.S. Capitol building. There were carved statues along the dark walls. The ceiling of the rotunda was at least fifty feet high. I stared wide-eyed at the mural someone had painted on the ceiling.

A cluster of students walked by me, eyeing me curiously, either because of my limp or because I was new. I tried not to stare back, but I estimated that their outfits cost more than the beater Ford truck I'd driven to school today.

The girls in the group looked like they'd just gotten a blowout at the salon across the road, and the guys looked like they belonged in an Abercrombie catalog.

I forced myself not to fidget with the plain black long-sleeved tee from Walmart I was wearing. This morning when I tried it on with the fake leather knee-length skirt that I'd found at a thrift store to go with it, I'd thought I looked great.

Now, I wasn't so sure.

All of the girls were wearing high heels; I had on a pair of black flats. It wasn't very practical...or safe for me to try and wear any kind of heels with the way my left foot dragged a bit. I also wanted to be prepared just in case Jackson had me running for my life once he saw me.

Well, hobbling for it anyway.

That last time we had seen each other...

It had been terrible.

I breathed a sigh of relief when I found a sign pointing in the direction of the Admissions Office. I followed the arrows until I found the glass-encased office. Pushing open the door, I cringed when I ran smack into someone.

"Ooof," I cried out as the bag I'd been holding tumbled to the floor. I was about to follow it when a strong set of hands caught me. Looking up, all I saw was green at first. The boy who'd caught me had the greenest eyes of anyone I'd ever seen.

"Hi," he said with a smug smile as he carefully helped me steady myself.

"Thank you," I breathed, trying to calm my pounding heart. I hadn't needed that extra shot of adrenaline. My espresso earlier had been enough.

"You're new," he commented, eyeing me up and down appreciatively before finally letting me go.

He was attractive, just like everyone else I had seen at this school. He had russet-colored hair to showcase those amazing green eyes of his, and he had to be at least six feet tall with a body that looked good, even under his clothes.

I watched him for a second, hoping that I would feel something, some small glimmer of attraction.

But like every guy I had seen since I was eight, my heart didn't even twitch.

I was impossibly fractured. Jackson Parker had cast some kind of spell on me and I wasn't sure that it would ever be broken.

It sank in, awkwardly, that the green-eyed hottie still stared at me. He had said something, but like the awkward turtle that I was, I had completely spaced it and missed what he said.

"Sorry...what?" I stuttered and he gave me a bemused

smile like he wasn't used to girls not paying rapt attention to every word that came out of his mouth.

"I asked what your name was," he said, amused.

"Everly," I stated, intentionally not giving him my last name. He would hear about who I was soon, and then he wouldn't want anything to do with me. "What's yours?" I quickly added so he wouldn't ask me to give it to him.

"Landry Evans," he replied, as if he expected me to know who he was.

Whoops. It was a defect that I needed to remedy. For too long, the only people I had cared about were Jackson and Caiden.

You would think that would have changed over the last two years.

"Nice to meet you," I finally answered, aware again of the awkward pause we'd just had while he waited for me to recognize him.

His amused grin grew wider. He had only seemed a little interested when I'd first bumped into him, but now the look in his eyes was almost feral.

It was a little unsettling.

"I'm the captain of the hockey team," he explained, still apparently waiting for that recognition to hit me.

I shrugged awkwardly. The only sport I followed was football, and that was only because the twins had forced it down my throat almost since the moment they'd met me until I loved it almost as much as they did. Both of them had played it and watched it 24/7, ensuring that I would have a steady diet of it.

I hadn't, nor would I ever, tell anyone how I'd spent every home game last season hovering outside the gates of the Rutherford Academy stadium...listening to the sounds of the game while I watched it on my cell phone, silently cheering Jackson on.

My heart throbbed painfully when I thought about the fact that the Dallas Cowboys had won the Superbowl last year, winning for the first time since 1997. They had been Caiden's favorite team and he, obviously, had missed it.

I took a deep breath.

"Well, I'm just going to get my schedule," I told him as I reached for my bag, as awareness of how close we were standing to each other hit me.

He rocked back on his heels, a little disappointment settling on his face. Maybe he realized I wasn't experiencing whatever connection he was.

"I could show you around?" he offered, once again shooting me that winsome grin.

"That's so nice, but I believe they've already assigned me someone to act as my class guide today. I really appreciate it though." I fought to sound earnest, while at the same time, beginning to push past him to get in the office. His face fell into a look of dismay.

He seemed to shake himself out of it though, and he started to back away, not taking his attention off of me and not bothering to look behind him to see if he was going to run into anyone. I had a feeling that things often went his way around here. He reminded me a little bit of Jackson, in that Jackson always put out that he had this outrageous confidence that everyone liked him and everyone would do as he said.

I was the only one who knew that was a lie.

"I'll be seeing you, Everly," he told me, and rather than sound like a goodbye, it sounded like a promise.

He would learn I wasn't the kind of girl you should make promises to.

I gave a half-hearted wave goodbye, and then I turned and finally made it into the Admissions' Office.

A stern-looking, grey-haired woman grimaced when she saw me approaching the counter. Looking down at my phone, I realized that Landry had cost me ten minutes that I didn't have.

Damn, I muttered to myself as I straightened my clothes and shot Ms. Grump a hopefully friendly smile.

She didn't seem impressed.

"Everly James," I announced politely. "Today's my first day."

"Class starts in ten minutes, Ms. James," she huffed with a shake of her head. "You would think you wouldn't want to be late on your first day," she continued as she began to type feverishly on her keyboard.

I didn't bother answering her that I'd tried to be early. Things just had a way of constantly going wrong in my life.

Ever heard of Murphy's Law? I was pretty sure that it should actually be called "Everly's Law" because I had never heard of someone having more bad luck than me.

"Do you have your license, Ms. James?" she asked loudly, and I realized that once again, I'd missed what someone said to me. I was really going to have to get myself together and pay attention. Unlike my old school, Rutherford Academy wasn't the kind of place where you could get away with spacing out and thinking about how much your life sucked.

That was probably a good thing for me.

I handed her my license, and she sniffed loudly as if my very presence offended her. Or maybe it was because unlike the rest of the student population here, who most likely housed their licenses in Louis Vuitton wallets...my wallet was something I had made myself using duct tape and safety pins. It had seemed cool when I'd made it. Or maybe that was just because Jackson used to have one just like it...

She held the license out to me with two fingers, most likely already envisioning how soon she could wash her hands. I took it back quickly, waiting quietly as she started to print out papers. Looking around the room, it was apparently I'd caught the attention of the entire office. Some of the employees were watching me unabashedly. It made me wish once again that I'd been able to start last week with the rest of the students. Even though I was new, I wouldn't have stood out so much.

Mom getting drunk and falling down a flight of stairs hadn't been in the cards.

But, again...not much in my life was.

"Here you go," the woman said sharply, handing me a black folder emblazoned with the Rutherford Academy crest in the center. "You'd better hurry. You have two minutes before the bell rings," she muttered, before turning her attention back to her computer like I didn't exist.

"Aren't I supposed to have a student guide?" I asked, looking around to see if anyone looked like they were waiting for me.

"Get to class, Ms. James," she said in a bored tone, completely ignoring me.

"Thanks," I responded, just barely succeeding in keeping the annoyance out of my voice.

I walked out the door, back into the hallway.

And suddenly, there *he* was.

A rush of adrenaline hit me. I thought I had remembered how beautiful he was, but the memory and the pictures that I had didn't do him justice. Especially this new, older version of Jackson. The structure of his face was like a work of art, the planes and angles so geometrically perfect that he was a flesh and blood sculpture. His golden skin fit across his bones like a glove, a piece of satin stretched taut. His blonde hair was perfectly tousled, not long enough to be feminine, but long enough to attract all things feminine. I looked up at his beautiful face, his shockingly blue eyes and strong jaw, just the perfect amount of stubble softening the angles. His broad shoulders beckoned to me, and the smooth skin of his hard chest was visible above the collar of his shirt.

Everything about him called to me.

Have you ever felt it? The change in the air around you? That essential change in the tides? The way the sun suddenly seemed like it rose and set with only one person in mind. Maybe it didn't happen for everyone, maybe it was just me. But the feeling when you know your life will absolutely never be the same again—I'd only felt that twice before. The day my father killed himself, and the day I first met Jackson Parker on the playground.

Now, seeing Jackson again? That feeling engulfed me and took my breath away. It was a tingle in my toes, a warmth in my stomach. Wet burned my eyes, and I fought it, like people always did when they were scared, but it won.

My heart sped up to beat wildly. Especially when he looked up. He walked towards me, and the fluttering inside my stomach intensified. Was this going to be it? Were we just going to reconnect right now as easily as that? Had he finally forgiven me?

He was five feet away when I realized that he was focused on someone behind me. He walked past me like I didn't exist, even though he had to have seen me. I turned around to watch him go, very aware that many of the other people in the hallway were also watching him, despite the fact that the bell was going to ring any minute.

Then he strode over to a beautiful girl with auburn colored hair and pulled her into his arms, beginning to make-out with her right there in the hallway.

He might as well have just punched me. Because it might have been kinder than how it felt as he devoured the pretty girl's lips.

It was awful, and it transported me back to that last night I'd seen him and the cruel words he'd spoken.

Suddenly, the rosy picture I painted for myself of what life was going to be like at Rutherford Academy went up in smoke.

An arm slung over my shoulder and I startled at the unexpected touch. Looking to my left, I found a girl with raven-colored hair, bright blue and green streaks colorfully woven throughout it. She was dressed in a pair of artfully torn skinny jeans and a vintage Ramones t-shirt. I only said vintage because people didn't seem to like the Ramones very much nowadays. My father had fed me a steady diet of rock-n-roll when he wasn't stealing from people, and so I appreciated her shirt. The stranger smacked a piece of gum and watched the Jackson show with an amused smirk.

"Oh, don't tell me the Heartbreak Prince has already caught your eye. That doesn't bode well for you," she commented dryly in a delightfully raspy voice.

I shrugged her arm off me, my cheeks coloring with embarrassment.

"Who are you?" I asked with a frown. I needed to get to class but I seemed trapped and unable to keep my gaze from flicking back to Jackson, who'd thankfully finally stopped devouring the girl's mouth.

"You're new today, right?" the girl next to me asked, grabbing my attention again as she stared me up and down. "The school's not that big, and I know I would've noticed you before if you'd started with the rest of the new juniors last week."

"I'm—" I began.

"Oh, I haven't introduced myself. That's why this is awkward," she said with a sly grin, extending a hand that was laden with different sized rings. "I'm Lane," she explained. "And you need to relax. I've just been messing with you. Admissions sent me to show you around. I assumed you were the new student, since I hadn't seen you before."

I let out a little sigh of relief that one of the first people I talked to in the school hadn't ended up being a crazy person. Although, I guess that really remained to be seen.

I extended my hand. "Everly."

She shot me a sneaky grin and then shook my hand. After letting go, she pulled a folder out of the blue satchel she was carrying. My name was on it. "Let's take a look at your schedule and get you to class. There's not much we can do for you to be on time for this first one, but hopefully you won't get too hard of a time. The professors here are kind of crazy about punctuality. Although you would think with the amount of money that we're paying, they would work around our schedule," she said with another smirk.

The hallway had become a ghost town. Jackson and everyone else had disappeared in the minute I'd been talking to Lane. I ignored the flicker of hurt singing my insides that Jackson hadn't even bothered to say a word to me.

I would have taken even a hateful word after two years of harsh silence.

The bell chose that moment to ring.

Lane began walking as she examined a piece of paper she'd pulled from the folder. She made a few noises as she examined it. "Looks like we have a little smarty on her hands," she commented. "Half of your classes are with the freshman. We even have British literature together."

My mood improved marginally. At least I would have one class with someone I knew. I dreaded the freshman classes the most, even though they were on topics that interested me because there was a greater chance that I would be in a class with Jackson.

"Okay, I'll show you to AP Biology. It's in the next building," she explained as she started to walk quickly. I followed after her.

She pointed out some things along the way, like one of the three cafeterias that the school possessed. Rutherford also had two coffee shops, a pizzeria, a Japanese/sushi joint, and a burger place. It all seemed a bit much considering there was only around five hundred students in the junior and senior grades and fifteen hundred people in each college class...but what did I know?

Lane directed my attention to one hallway where the various football offices were. Beyond the double doors at the end of the hallway was the main athletic complex along with the giant stadium that could seat forty thousand people. Although the school was small, the alumni base was so strong, and the football team so good, that the school had built a new stadium about five years before. Games were always sold out, even with that many seats, and there was talk of expanding the stadium in the near future to hold even more.

Of course every time I thought of football, I thought of Jackson. How could I not when he'd been playing since he was in sixth grade? He was currently the star wide receiver on the team, even as a freshman, and he deserved all the hype. He was magic on the field.

Just like he was everywhere else.

Lane looked at another piece of paper as we walked and let out a small squeal that made me stumble, not something that was difficult to do with how much my foot was dragging today. I'd noticed early on after the accident that my symptoms seemed to be aggravated whenever I was particularly nervous...or when the weather was bad.

I liked Lane even more when she pretended not to notice.

My limp wasn't huge, but it was impossible to miss, and I'd had people tell me over the last two years how tragic it was that I'd sustained such a flaw in an otherwise perfect physical appearance.

Because all the other things that happened because of the accident weren't tragic, right?

My limp was really a small thing in the grand scheme of the horrors created that night.

"You're in the Baker dorm," she said when I recovered from almost falling. "That's my dorm. It's a good one. We don't get single rooms, but there's only two people per room, and the rooms come with their own private bathroom."

Even though I lived only an hour away, I had chosen to take advantage of the living accommodations that came with my scholarship. Chosen was probably not the right word, I had been desperately excited to accept the offer to live somewhere other than with my mother. The school representative I'd spoken to over the summer had explained that most of the students chose to live on campus, but I hadn't cared about that. I would have accepted the offer, even if it meant I had to live in a van down by the river for my accommodations.

We exited the main building and walked across a large green crisscrossed with various concrete walking paths. All of the buildings surrounding the green looked like structures you would have found in ancient Rome, all Corinthian columns and white marble. It was like I had stepped into a dream. Only my presence here convinced me that it was real, because my brain would never have created such a good dream.

I only had nightmares when I slept.

"I'll meet you after your class and show you to the dorms. Looks like you have about thirty minutes in between this class and the next. Is your stuff in your car?"

I nodded absentmindedly, still a little awestruck at how beautiful this place was. I'd gone on a tour of the campus with the twins before everything happened when we'd all been determined to attend together...not that the twins were ever in danger of not attending. The harshness of the past few years had faded the brilliance of the campus from my mind. It was a testament to how hard my life had been that I could forget how amazing this place was.

"Do we need to find some hotties to help lug all your stuff in?" she asked, and with that question, my cheeks burst into flames as I thought about how little I'd brought with me.

I didn't even have enough stuff to warrant Lane helping me, but I guess she could carry a backpack if she really wanted to help.

"I think I'll be okay," I told her as we entered what Lane said was the science building where my first class was located. I was about ten minutes late now and dreading every step closer to the class that I walked. It was going to be really fun to walk in and get everyone's attention. Especially since biology was one of the freshman classes I was taking.

"Sure you don't want me to ask Jackson Parker to help?" she teased. And just like that, all of my blush rushed out of my face. "Shit...I was just joking," she quickly said at my horrified face. "Parker wouldn't help me even if I begged him to. I'm not at His Majesty's level, and I won't ever be," she added a bit bitterly.

I didn't comment. Jackson had always been like that, always the most popular kid, but only choosing to keep to a few people in his friend group, and only considering Caiden and me as his best friends. Everyone else didn't exist as far as he'd been concerned.

When would it stop feeling so weird that I was now one of those people that didn't exist for him?

Probably never.

I shook it off as we stopped in front of the tall double doors that led into the lecture hall. "I'll go in with you. I took biology as a senior last year with Professor Jones and she loves me," Lane stated confidently as she quietly opened the doors and walked in.

I sighed a little as we walked in. This was a huge class, and we were entering from the back, left side of the enormous room. At least a few hundred students were in here, and the lights were dimmed as the professor lectured about something showing on the huge projector screen. She didn't even spare us a glance as I quickly found a seat and only a few other students even looked at me.

Lane gave me a thumbs up before leaving as silently as we'd come in. I felt a little naked without her beside me, like she had been shielding me.

It was stupid, but I immediately knew that Jackson wasn't in this class. And I didn't know whether to be relieved or disappointed.

I hated how much I thought about him, even after all this time and everything he'd said to me. I just couldn't kick him out of my head...or really my heart for that matter. It was like he'd taken up residence years ago and decided never to move out.

Shaking my head, I pulled out the computer that had come with my scholarship and began to take notes, quickly recognizing the professor was lecturing on cell structure. Throwing all my attention to the screen she was lecturing on, I once again promised myself that my past wasn't going to affect my future.

One way or another, I was going to succeed here. Jackson Parker be damned.

JUST AS SHE'D PROMISED, Lane was waiting for me after class. I'd gotten a few more looks as everyone began exiting the classroom, but the fact that they were just curious looks had me counting my first class as a win.

We managed to walk to our dormitory without seeing Jackson, and I considered myself a little luckier than I had been earlier. I was even letting myself think about how much I loved the school already.

And then I met my roommate.

I could feel Lane freeze next to me when I pulled out my key and opened the door on who I assumed was my roommate...butt naked under some guy.

"Get *out*," she screamed as her "friend" tried to pull a blanket over his naked ass.

Lane and I quickly left the room, slamming the door behind us as we stood in the hallway horrified.

"They didn't tell me you were rooming with her," Lane said with a groan, slumping against the hallway as if she'd just been delivered the worst news ever.

"Who is she?" I asked, really wanting to douse my eyeballs in bleach after what I'd just seen.

I really couldn't think of a worse introduction to my roommate.

Well, I guess she could have been mid-thrust with Jackson. That would have been unrecoverable.

"That was Melanie Carmichael. She's a cheerleader. Thinks her shit doesn't stink," Lane explained. "She's going to hate you." Lane looked me up and down. "She hates people prettier than her."

I rolled my eyes at the compliment and had just opened my mouth to say something when the door opened and a cocky stunner of a guy with bright orange hair left the room, shooting me a wink as he passed. I kept my eyes averted from his form as he left. It would be a while before I would forget the sight of his thrusting ass.

He obviously worked out.

My new roommate poked her head out, an annoyed look on her face as she gave me a quick glance up and down.

"Well, come in," she snapped. Lane gave me a look before gesturing me inside. I was suddenly grateful I would need to leave soon to get to my next class.

Melanie was a pretty girl. A bottle blonde with a perfect figure and soft blue eyes, she looked exactly like what I would envision a cheerleader at this school would look like.

While Melanie intentionally ignored me and straightened her bed, I looked around my new room.

It was much nicer than my room back home. It was huge, easily fitting two queen beds on either side of the room along with two desks, two dressers, a large cream rug, and a tv stand complete with a big screen.

We'd long ago run out of money to pay for cable, so

without the twins in my life anymore, I hadn't done a lot of TV watching the last few years.

There were a few doors on one side of the room. I assumed there were two closets and a bathroom behind them.

Lane had been right. It sucked to share a room, but the room itself was nice.

"You must be my new roomie," Melanie suddenly said, and it was like someone had possessed her body because her voice had suddenly become incredibly sweet and welcoming.

I shook her hand when she held out hers for me to take.

"Everly James," I introduced myself as I shifted shyly under her gaze. I'd never gotten along with girls particularly well, Lane being an outlier at the moment. They'd always been trying to be friends with me to get closer to the guys, and I hadn't felt I really needed anyone but them.

This was going to be a learning curve for me.

"Melanie Carmichael," she responded, dropping my hand and stepping away from me, once again examining me closely. "But I'm sure Lane told you all about me," she added snottily, shooting Lane a glare, who just shrugged while giving her a big "Fuck You" grin in return.

"Listen, as long as you stay out of my way and aren't a slob, we won't have any issues. Give me your cell phone number so I can let you know when I have visitors," she added, holding out her hand expectantly.

I stared at her a bit dismayed before pulling out my iPhone that was at least five years old. Melanie looked at it as if it was a poop-filled diaper before reluctantly grabbing it and punching in her number.

"I'm texting myself so I have your number," she said

before typing a few more things into my phone and handing it back.

There was a large mirror by her bed, and she peered into it briefly, straightening her cobalt blue jersey dress that showed off her thin form. She gave herself an approving stare that was a bit awkward to watch.

"I've got to get to class. Later," she threw at me suddenly before slipping into a pair of leopard booties, grabbing her Louis Vuitton purse, and exiting the room without a look back.

I stared at Lane, my mouth hanging open with a bit of shock.

She just grinned at me.

"Welcome to Rutherford," she sang at me.

Well, shit.

Only News, Never Opinions.   11 August

Dayton Valley News

Your Best Source of News Since 1965

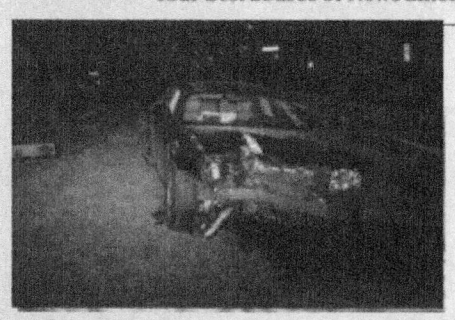

Car Accident Injures Two. High School Football Star in Critical Condition.

Caiden Parker, South High's Star Tight End was in a car accident on Friday at around two am with an unidentified female. Parker's car was found wrapped around a traffic light. There were no other cars involved in the accident. Parker was life flighted to Memorial Hospital where he is said to be under critical condition. Parker's companion was also taken to Memorial and has been in and out of surgeries. A hospital spokesperson declined to make a statement due to the age of the minors involved. Parker's family, a well-known institution in Dayton is said to be in hysterics. Mr. Parker's twin, Parker Jackson, is also a local star.

Story continued on A2.

Carrolton Flyers Ready To Make Their Mark As Soccer Season Begins.

The Carrolton Flyers are set to make their debut on August 15th. Pre-season play started three weeks ago and the Flyers emerged with a record of 3-2. "We think we're going to have a great season this year," commented Team O'Neil, the Flyers goalie and captain of six years. Story continued on A5.

4

THEN

My name was Everly James, and I was a con man's daughter. And not just any con man, but the con man who'd lost millions of our town's money and then shot his brains out on the front sidewalk when the feds came for him in a bloody ending that the town would never forget.

There was no one in this city, let alone the state, who was hated more.

And my mother refused to move.

Shannon James was a proud woman. One who had grown accustomed to the riches and privilege my dad had provided her. So accustomed, in fact, that when she found out years before how my father was making his money, she didn't tell him to stop.

Of course for the past few years, she'd been trying to play the victim, telling anyone who would listen that she'd been just as taken with my father's smooth words and gorgeous looks as everyone else.

In my mind, she was worse than him.

Despite her attempt for pity, she'd lost all of her friends, all of her money, and she would've lost the house too if my father hadn't put it in her name and made sure it was paid off before he offed himself.

So ironically, we lived in a mansion that badly needed repairs and staff, but my mama refused to give it up and sell it so we actually had money for things like...groceries, clothes...necessities of life.

That didn't mean that she didn't sell some of her fancy items. But it certainly wasn't to clothe or feed me. Pieces of jewelry Daddy had given her went first, and then priceless artwork would disappear off the walls to pay for alcohol or to put gas in her car. When she remembered to get groceries, she would always buy ridiculous things like caviar and champagne, something that a six-year-old was obviously not going to eat. When she remembered, she would buy me a loaf of generic white bread and some peanut butter, and that was how I'd get by. That was why starting school, I was not only the smallest kid in the class, but also the most hated and ridiculed, even though I had nothing to do with my asshole of a father's actions.

To make life worse, my father's death somehow pushed my mother to a point where she no longer could stand the sight of my face. She didn't love me anymore. In fact, I would go so far to say that she hated me. If my shoes even squeaked on the floors of the house, I'd be thrown in a closet for the rest the day, or lashed repeatedly with one of my father's belts.

When she was really drunk, I scared her. Probably because I looked like my father. His curly gold hair and catlike green eyes stared back at me in the mirror every time I looked into one. The combination had been what made my father so hard to say no to. He looked so charming and innocent, certainly not the face of someone who was going to rob you blind. There was no way for me to hide from everyone around town that I wasn't my father's daughter.

In short, my life was hell. The worst kind of hell.

I was fruit, ripe for the taking for the Parker brothers. They offered me the warmth, love, and attention I was desperate for. They were my greatest loves, and my worst mistakes.

I should've chosen better from the start, I should've recognized that although I loved Caiden, it wasn't the soul crushing kind of love I felt for Jackson.

I should have done so many things differently.

5

NOW

Jackson

I fell in love with Everly James the first time that I saw her on that playground, holding her ground against kids twice her size. She was tiny, her tangled curly blonde hair so long and thick that it practically covered her face. When I saw her standing there so bravely, all I could think was she was the most beautiful creature that I'd ever seen.

There was only one other person I loved as much.

And that was Caiden.

I was fucked up.

Even as a kid, I couldn't control my emotions. The slightest things would set me off. My mom would tell me that I needed to eat the vegetables on my plate, and next thing I knew, the plate would be shattered against the wall, the spaghetti that had been on the same plate sliding down the wall leaving an oily, red stain that would have to be painted over. My dad told us to turn off my favorite movie and a baseball trophy would find its way to the television screen minutes later, glass shattering all over the carpeted game room.

They tried all the parenting tricks they could find. Grounding me, taking away toys, trying to bribe me. Nothing worked. Except for Caiden.

When the anger built up inside of me, I couldn't think straight. It felt like the real me was locked inside, a slave to the darkness and frustration that I couldn't get past. Caiden was always there, soothing me, talking me down from the ledge I was poised to jump off of. It only ingratiated it more for my parents. He was the golden child, the peacemaker, the better twin.

I loved him too much to be jealous of him.

Doctors told my parents it was ADHD, intermittent explosive disorder, too much sugar, not enough sleep. The list went on and on. I was put on various diets, medicines, therapies...but the hyper manic behavior...the irrational anger...it continued.

The depression didn't set in until later.

And that was when I got my final diagnosis.

Bipolar.

It was kind of an ironic thing. How being bipolar made sure that I would always be more popular than Caiden. My manic episodes made me loud and brash, willing to do anything, unafraid of the world. The kids gravitated towards me, not seeing the days when I couldn't get out of bed, when Caiden had to sleep next to me because I couldn't stop crying.

I saw it in my parents' eyes now, after the accident, the fact that they could barely look at me.

They wished it was me lying in that hospital bed.

And I didn't blame them.

I wished it was me as well.

And it was all her fault.

For two brothers who'd always been inseparable, it sure took us a long time to realize that the both of us were in love with the same girl. I marched into Everly's life in my usual way, not thinking of consequences or anything else for that matter. I saw those green eyes, those pouty lips on that angelic face.

And I wanted her.

Only turned out that my brother did, too.

I brushed a hand down my face, still tasting the egg burrito that Jadin must have eaten for breakfast. I was sure she would have at least chewed some gum if she knew I was going to jump her like that. I hadn't touched Jadin in ages. I had a one-fuck rule. But I'd panicked when I saw Everly standing there, the loveliest pain you could imagine.

Shame soured my stomach because even after everything that had happened, even after what she'd done to Caiden...what *we'd* done to Caiden, I still wanted her.

After enough time passed, I began to think that I couldn't possibly have imagined something so perfect. I'd burned nearly all the pictures of us, especially the pictures of the three of us. And I'd told myself that there was no way I was remembering the slope of her nose right, or the way her eyes seemed to sparkle when she laughed, or how smooth her skin felt under my hands. Sometimes I told myself that I'd imagined she was so perfect just to hurt myself, to punish myself for the part I'd played in my brother's downfall.

But seeing her today...I realized that if anything, I'd remembered her as less perfect than she really was. I understood now why it had hurt so much. Because the kind of pain I'd been experiencing couldn't exist if she hadn't been real.

She was the devil hidden behind an angel's face, and I was so fucking tired of the temptation of her. I hated her in a way that sometimes still shocked me.

Because as much as I hated her.

I couldn't forget that I'd once loved her more.

I had spent the last two years cursing her name, happy for the reprieve from seeing her face and remembering over and over what we'd done to my brother.

EVERLY

Sharing a room with Melanie was going to be awkward. And that was probably an understatement.

I had come back from a blissfully Jackson-free dinner with Lane in one of the cafeterias to find that she'd rifled through my stuff. She didn't even bother to put things back. Everything was scattered around on the floor, wrinkled and stepped on. She lay on her stomach on her bed, watching an episode of *Gossip Girl* when I walked in, and even though I was sure that she knew I was looking at her wondering what the fuck she'd done to my stuff...she didn't even turn her head to look at me.

She couldn't hide that miniscule little smirk though.

That told me I wasn't going to be finding refuge in my room any time soon. It was good that I didn't have much by way of earthly possessions, and that my journal was still hidden in my car. Because it was clear that Melanie was the type to rifle through a journal and probably post all the juicy parts around the dorms for good measure.

I didn't know if I was relieved or not that our "private bathroom" actually only consisted of a private toilet and mirror. I was still going to have to use the common area showers. I knew I would never have felt comfortable showering while Melanie was in the room though, and at least the common area showers had outside doors that could be locked, even if someone could peek in from over and under the doors.

I waited until Melanie was asleep before I snuck out to the showers with my caddie. The common rooms were blissfully quiet. I hadn't expected anyone to be friendly, having one friend like Lane was more than I'd thought I'd get, but the looks from the girls that I'd seen so far had been downright hostile.

It had been ten years since my father had gone out with a bang...but it still seemed like the memory of his sins wasn't fading, even towns away.

I'm used to being hated.

I'm used to being lonely.

Someday, I would get far enough away from my past that it could no longer haunt me.

Ignoring the image of Jackson's perfect face floating through my mind every time I thought of leaving this state for good and the pang of regret that image always brought me, I focused on what was in front of me, what needed to be done.

I showered quickly, the blissful quiet transforming into eerie silence for some reason. I'd brought my pajamas with me, not daring to make the rookie mistake of going down the hall with just a towel on in the off chance that someone was out there ready to make a fool of me.

After I was dressed, I crept down the halls, back to my room. I kept the lights off while I put my caddie away, trying to be as quiet as possible so that I didn't wake Melanie up...she was, unfortunately, a bit of a snorer. But I guess I would always know when she was asleep.

I sunk down on my bed, immediately letting out a small shriek as soon as my body touched my sheets.

They were soaking wet with chunks of ice scattered all over.

Someone—my new roommate most likely—had dumped ice water all over my bed.

My shriek had been loud enough to raise the dead, but my roommate hadn't even budged, and the sounds of her snoring were still there.

Evidently, she was an actress as well.

I started shaking, not knowing how to describe exactly what I experienced; maybe it was a mixture of anger and distress.

No matter where I went, or how "elite" or "mature" the student body was supposed to be...it was still going to be like this.

I was exhausted and now I had nowhere to sleep. My roommate...or whoever had done this, had done a good job, there wasn't a spot of my bed that had been untouched. I guess I should just be happy that it was just water and not something worse.

This was a warning shot, to remind me where exactly my place was in this school. For a moment, I longed for Jackson. He'd always been my protector growing up and it was a bad habit that I still wished he was in that role.

Scooping up my pillow and setting it down on the floor, I put a few layers of my clothes on top of it, hoping they would keep me from feeling the worst of the chilly dampness. I couldn't risk going to sleep out on the couches out in the common room, and I didn't know where Lane's room was yet. I just had to hope that my roommate didn't decide to draw on my face while I was sleeping.

It was a long night, and Melanie made sure to step on my hair in the morning when she woke up for class, pretending that she hadn't seen me there.

"Why exactly are you sleeping on the floor?" she said in an annoyed voice, no sign on her face that she was the culprit behind my wet night.

I opened my mouth to respond and then decided against it. There was no way that she one, somehow missed someone either coming into the room and dumping water all over my bed...or two, forgot she had decided to torture her new roommate for kicks and giggles.

"Rough mattress," I finally answered, a dare in my eye as I stared at her. Her eyes widened imperceptibly, a little grin flashing on her face before she flounced into the bathroom without another word.

When she didn't come out after twenty minutes, it dawned on me I wasn't going to make it to class on time if I waited to get ready when she was done.

Flipping open my compact mirror, I groaned. I looked like shit. I guess that's what sleeping on the floor on a soggy pillow with one eye open did to you.

Half a bottle of concealer, and I knew it wasn't going to get any better. Giving up, I put a little eyeliner and mascara and some pink lip-gloss, and called it good. My hair went up in a messy bun. My roommate had every outlet taken over in the bedroom, and I didn't feel like inciting her wrath by unplugging something she thought important to use my hair straightener.

That was a fight for another day.

Some black skinny jeans and a black spaghetti strap top followed by an oversized flannel completed my look. Not what I would have picked for my second day at Rutherford, but there were worse things.

A wave of guilt hit me just then, so strong that it threatened to knock me over with its suddenness. Here I was worrying about stupid things like how I looked...and Caiden wouldn't ever get to care about anything again.

I drew in a hiccupping breath, practicing my deep breathing exercises that my hospital mandated therapist had taught me when my anxiety attacks after Caiden's accident crippled me.

After a few minutes, my panic subsided, and I was able to breathe normally.

I glanced at my phone. *Shit,* I was going to be late.

I walked out of my room, down the hall, and out of the dorm, my limp more pronounced after my uncomfortable night on the floor. I rubbed my thigh, hoping that the pain shooting through my leg would subside soon. I needed to pop an Advil as soon as I got to class.

I was a few feet away from my dorm room door when a familiar face suddenly popped up beside me.

"Hey, dollface," Landry said. He was wearing a tight-fitting forest green Henley that made his amazing green eyes pop even more. He was a nice sight after the night I'd just had.

"Can I take you to breakfast?" he asked, taking my book bag off my shoulder and hoisting it onto his own. I hadn't dared to leave any of my books in my room with Melanie, not sure what she or someone else would do to them so they were all in my bag, making my limp even worse under the weight.

"Did you pack rocks in here?" he asked, pretending to hunch over from the weight of my bag.

"Something like that," I murmured, not wanting to get into what had happened the night before. The verdict was still out for Landry, and there was no way I was spilling anything important to him right now.

"So...breakfast?" he asked again, and I gave him a small frown of disappointment.

"Unfortunately, my roommate hogged the bathroom this morning, and I'm running late," I told him as we began to walk towards where I hoped I was right that my classes were.

He looked so disappointed that I decided to throw him a bone. "I could meet you for lunch?" I told him, wishing that his green eyes stirred up even an ounce of lust. I really needed to find a way to unbreak myself.

Speaking of lust, I caught sight just then of Jackson, talking with a group of guys that looked like they were on the football team with him, judging by their size. He talked to them, but his gaze was locked on mine. It was the first time we'd had any form of eye contact in years and I worried I was going to melt on the spot. By his mere presence, Jackson Parker commanded attention, and he definitely had mine; every nerve in my body was highly attuned to his proximity, shimmering like a spark waiting to ignite. His intense gaze held mine for what felt like an eternity before Landry asked me something that forced me to look away.

I thought Landry had just asked me what class I had today, but I wasn't paying attention. Landry threw a frown over my shoulder, aimed at Jackson.

He chose to ignore my distraction, repeating his question again with a charming smile. I opened my mouth to answer when I felt *him*. Landry's mouth pursed in displeasure, and I turned around, trying to prepare myself for the experience of having Jackson so close to me.

"Can I help you, Parker?" Landry barked. Oh, they knew each other and apparently, they had bad blood between them because Jackson was shooting him a look that could kill.

"Just wanted to see who you had here, Evans," Jackson replied, his smooth voice rolling over my skin, sending an instant rush of lust skittering across my body. Jackson glanced at me casually, and I realized that he was going to pretend that he didn't know me. What was that all about?

"You must be the newbie," he said charmingly, holding out his hand. There was a low rumble behind me, and Jackson's cocky grin grew even wider. I stared at his hand for a moment, getting the feeling that it was going to bite me. Uncertain of what game Jackson wanted to play, I hesitated to involve myself. After it started to get awkward, I tentatively reached out my hand towards his.

As my palm connected with his, a line of electricity shot up my arm, and the air felt full of an almost palpable energy. His brow furrowed and his smirk dissolved into the straight line of his lips. Had he felt it, too? The intensity of his stare caused a hot flush to spread up my chest like a wildfire. Those damn eyes—it was as if they searched mine for answers to unasked questions. My lips parted to respond to the mysterious inquiry, but no sound escaped my now parched throat. Shaking my head, I recovered and slipped free from his grip.

With our physical connection broken, his smile returned.

"If there's anything you need, I'm Jackson, and I'm at your service," he told me.

I took a step backward, needing space from the energy

he threw at me. He followed my movements to my plain black flats. Suddenly, I didn't feel as ferocious as I had when I left my dorm room a few minutes earlier. The confidence I held as I slipped into my favorite flannel had been stripped away, leaving only me. Everly James, loser, traitor... cheater.

And in front of me was a god among men.

Jackson Parker wasn't the boy next door—he was the lion ready to slaughter the lamb. I counted to three to ensure I wouldn't squeak out an answer. "I think I'll be fine."

His eyes continued with their hypnotic spell as others invaded the moment, the group of guys he'd been talking to when I first saw him sidling up to where we were standing.

"Who do we have here?" one of them purred, looking me up and down in a way that made me immediately feel dirty.

Was it just my imagination or had Jackson just taken a step in front of me so he blocked me from view? That couldn't have been on purpose...right?

"Everly, you were saying you were running late for class?" Landry reminded me, and I nodded, shooting them all what I hoped looked like a polite smile, despite the fact that they were all looking at me like I was fresh meat.

Landry hustled me away from the group, but I could feel Jackson's hot stare following me as I walked. I thought a lot about what we would say to each other when he saw me again, but I hadn't anticipated what had just happened. It made me feel uneasy and a little sick to my stomach. Jackson had always been bold. I'd grown used to his antics after so many years as his best friend...but whatever game he'd just started with me? I didn't know how to handle that.

"...lunch?" Landry asked as we stopped in front of the building that housed my class.

I nodded numbly and waved to him as I hustled into the

grey stone building, desperate to get away from both Jackson's and Landry's stares.

It was hard to concentrate during class, even though the professor was engaging. It should have been one of my favorite classes—English literature, but all I could think about was that strange look in Jackson's eyes as he stared at me. Like he had plans for me...and not good ones.

No one tried to talk to me, and that was fine. The distrustful side-eyes directed my way were enough to deal with.

I hustled out of class, or, at least, went as fast as my leg would allow, suddenly eager to see Landry's friendly face. It was still way achier than usual, thanks to my night on my floor. Which reminded me, I needed to find Advil and find out where the school laundry was this afternoon so that I could wash my sheets. It hadn't smelled like anything but water, but I wasn't going to risk it, even if my budget hadn't anticipated needing to wash things this early on.

I got outside and squinted into the sunshine as I looked for Landry's face. There was no sign of him. I sat on one of the benches outside the building and waited.

After ten minutes, I felt like a fool. Landry wasn't here, and I was pretty sure that he wasn't coming.

Deciding I'd had enough, I got up to make my way to one of the cafeterias. Skipping breakfast had left me starving.

I made my way across the bustling green space, getting shoulder checked several times by other students as they walked by, not bothering to pay attention to where they were going, thanks to the fact that their eyes were glued to their phones.

When I'd made it across the green and there was still no sign of Landry, I pushed aside my disappointment and vowed to not accept any more lunch invitations with strangers.

My stomach growled, and I sped up my walk, I just needed to get through an alley in between two buildings that were in front of the cafeteria, and then I could eat.

I had just entered the alley when I stopped in surprise. Jackson leaned against the wall, by himself, as if waiting for me.

"Hi," I said cautiously, limping toward him. His eyes glittered as he watched my walk for a moment, but then they lifted back to my face and stared at me decidedly disinterested.

He pushed away from the wall and prowled towards me. I resisted the urge to run away, steeling my shoulders as he approached.

Of course, being Jackson, he couldn't stop at a respectable distance from me, he had to make sure he was up close, taking up all of my space.

"Not ignoring me now?" I asked, not liking how breathy my voice sounded as I spoke. It sounded far too affected.

"I wasn't ignoring you. I didn't recognize the whore standing in front of me out there," he said blithely as he once again flicked his gaze up and down my body.

I tried to throttle the hurt crashing over me at his words. He knew I wasn't a whore. He knew because he was the first...and only guy I'd ever been with. Not that he would know that last part now.

"What are you doing here?" he finally growled when I didn't respond to his bait.

"You know what I'm doing here," I said exasperatedly. "I toured the campus with you..." I stopped, my words getting caught in my throat since Caiden had also been there for that tour.

He took a step back, a triumphant look on his face, as if his whole goal in the conversation had been to remind me of Caiden, the boy I'd destroyed.

"Trust me when I tell you this is the last place you should be," he told me as he reached out and briefly touched a piece of my hair that had flown into my face. He pulled back his hand like he'd been stung, and I ignored the way I desperately craved his touch.

Raising his fingers to his mouth, he began to pull on his lower lip as he continued to stare at me, and as usual...it did something to me. The same something it did earlier this morning. I shifted, hoping he didn't notice my thighs squeezing together.

Of course he did, and his pensive stare changed to the cocky smirk that I was infinitely familiar with.

"Jackson, please..." I said, all my plans to play it cool disappearing now that he was standing in front of me.

For some reason, me saying his name angered him, and he suddenly grasped my chin so tightly that I was sure he would leave a bruise. "I told you two years ago that you were dead to me, Eves," he murmured, one of his pet names for me slipping out, accidently I was sure. "I haven't changed my mind. I'm warning you right now to leave...because I'm a nice guy," he continued, with a grin that was definitely not nice before he released my chin, turned, and began to walk away.

"Is that a threat?" I called in a clenched voice after him.

He laughed, the sound menacing and cold. "No, Everly. It's a promise," he threw over his shoulder before he turned the corner and disappeared from sight.

I resisted the urge to sink to my knees right here in the alley. A group of giggling girls walked past me at that moment, giving me strange looks since I was frozen in place in the middle of the walkway.

Like I said, I'd imagined different scenarios of how our first meeting would go constantly over the last two years.

But I hadn't imagined this.

6

JACKSON

I smirked as I spotted Landry across the room sporting the black eye I'd given him after this morning's meet and greet on the green. I'd heard that he'd been holed up in the trainer's office this morning getting checked out for a concussion. He had hit his head pretty hard after I punched him. Wouldn't want him to miss his hockey exhibition tonight.

Landry wouldn't squeal, that I was sure of. His pride was too big for that. And he knew the hit had just been a warning, a warning not to mess with what was mine. I just hoped that he'd gotten the message so I didn't have to give him another one.

I sighed and shifted back into my seat uncomfortably, ignoring the way the girls from the cheerleader team in front of me were trying to get my attention. Whoever told girls flicking their hair and pretending to drop things so that guys could see down their shirts was the way to go really needed to be shot.

The fact I was hard right now had nothing to do with

them...unfortunately. And everything to do with the little bitch who had decided to come back into my life.

The image of her standing in that alley, staring me down bravely flashed in my head. She'd been wearing one of my flannel shirts, my favorite one in fact. And it had messed with me.

A lot.

The professor droned on, but I didn't bother listening. We were in a class aptly nicknamed "Rocks for Jocks" since the class consisted of athletes and cheerleaders...most of who didn't give a damn about the geology of our fair state, but who knew they would get a good grade from it.

I was generally a good student, but it was nice to have an hour three times a week where I could zone out, maybe nap if I needed to.

But I certainly wasn't napping right now. Not thanks to the boner I'd been sporting ever since my run-in with Everly. Although could I really call it a run-in since I'd been waiting for her, thanks to her schedule I'd charmed from Admissions. I'd told myself that I'd gotten it so that I could avoid her and at least have fair warning if she was in any of my classes.

But that was a lie.

I'd been obsessed with Everly James forever. It was a sickness that I needed to get rid of by any means necessary.

By the end of this semester, I wanted to never have to see that snake's face at this school again.

The fact that I saw her in my dreams every night was already enough.

Everly

My appetite was gone after my run-in with Jackson, so I decided to make my way back to my dorm, determined to stay low until my next class. I just hoped that Melanie was out and about for the day. I wasn't in the mood to deal with her. There was a special hell for passive aggressive people, and I was getting the feeling that she was the queen of it.

"Everly," someone called out as I was almost to my dorm.

Turning, I found Lane hustling towards me, her blue and green streaked hair flying behind her as she jogged.

"How's your first day going?" she asked when she got to me, slightly out of breath.

I just shrugged, not sure how to put into words all the emotions I was feeling.

"That good, huh?" Lane asked, a concerned expression on her pretty face. She had layered on the black eyeliner today, but she pulled it off well. It made her hazel eyes stand out even more. "It will get better," she told me sympathetically as we made our way through the front doors of our dorm.

"It's always hard to be the new girl, no matter how old you get."

"Yeah, I'm sure that's it," I responded, wishing I could tell her about Jackson, but I didn't know her well enough for that. I had learned along the way that you didn't really ever know anyone, so trusting strangers was even harder for me than it should have been.

"Do you know where the laundry room is in the building?" I asked as we stopped in front of my door and I remembered the soiled sheets that were waiting for me inside.

"It's just in the basement. What were you up to last night, dirty girl?" she asked with an impish grin.

I sighed and told her the story of my wet sheets. By the end of my story, I liked Lane even more because she looked like she was ready to throw down.

"That girl is such a twitch," she growled, and I let out a snort at the term.

She looked at me with a smirk. "My mom's a women's studies professor at Wesley, which means that I've been told since birth that I couldn't use the 'B' word when referencing woman," she explained.

"She is such a twitch," I said with a smile as we walked into my room, and I began to strip my still damp sheets from the bed.

"Are you sure it's just water?" Lane asked, wrinkling her nose at my admittedly threadbare sheets.

"No," I said. "But I can't afford to replace them at the moment, so let's hope that the washers are good here."

I wanted to slap myself for saying that as soon as the words came out of my mouth, but Lane didn't act fazed that I'd just admitted to being super poor. Maybe Lane would be a keeper.

The laundry room was in the basement, its spotless condition either showing how early it was in the semester to be doing laundry or showing that most of the rich kids at the school sent out their clothes to be washed instead of doing it themselves.

Not wanting to risk leaving my sheets down here, we sat on the counters and got to know each other more while they washed.

Lane was from New Hampshire, and had been born in September just like me. She'd traveled to fifty-seven countries already, thanks to her parents' various projects, and that she had a little sister who was only two because her parents "drank too much wine one night and forgot a condom."

I managed to keep Lane talking the whole time so I only had to provide a little bit of information about myself. Despite how open-minded Lane seemed, I had no idea how she would respond when she found out about my illustrious family history, and I wasn't looking to hasten her education in all things Everly James. I'm sure that would happen any day now. I'd managed to lose a friend in every grade I'd attended. I'd just not cared after a while because I had Jackson and Caiden by my side.

When my laundry was done, we headed upstairs to my still blissfully Melanie-free room. It was a shame how much I disliked my roommate already.

With a class starting in fifteen minutes, making my bed would have to wait. I just hoped that they would still be dry when I came back.

"British literature is today," Lane said brightly as I grabbed my book bag. "We have that together."

I perked up at that thought, and we headed to class after I securely locked the door behind me.

We were almost to class when someone called my name again. Landry ambled toward us, one of his eyes sporting a black and blue bruise that had not been there when I saw him this morning.

"What happened to you?" I gasped as he reached us. Lane glared at my handsome friend like he'd spit in her water. Landry didn't seem to notice as his gaze was locked on me.

"Sorry I missed lunch," he apologized. "I had an unexpected injury."

Lane snorted. "You mean Jackson Parker got you with his left-hook..." she clarified as Landry's face turned annoyed.

Shocked, I swung my gaze to her. "What did you just say?"

"Everly—" Landry began.

"Sorry, lover boy. But we've got class," Lane sang as she dragged me into our building, leaving a disgruntled looking Landry behind us. I waved at him sheepishly and then turned back to Lane, determined to get to the bottom of what she'd just said.

"I can't believe you didn't hear about it," Lane said excitedly, saving me from having to press her for information. "Everyone's talking about it. Jackson and Landry have always butted heads, but evidently, Jackson cornered him before class this morning and hit him so hard that Landry lost consciousness briefly."

My eyes widened. "Do you know why?" I prodded as we took seats in the back of the room.

"No one does," Lane explained, shaking her head. "Jackson's known for being a wild card, but that was a little far for even him."

I nodded my head, dazed, trying to quell the hope building in my chest that Jackson's reaction had something to do with Landry's interest in me.

Lane continued to chat about something else, but she'd lost me. My attention was firmly on Jackson and Landry.

I managed to pay attention in class though, which was good since I couldn't afford not to as my scholarship depended on near perfect grades. The professor was engaging, and the book list held some of my very favorites. British lit was going to be one of my favorite classes for sure.

I'd fallen in love with the written word when I'd discovered early on that most of my tormentors had no interest in reading...which meant that the town's library could be a haven for me. Ms. Buckland, the librarian, didn't seem to mind me, and she always pointed me to books I needed to read.

That was one of the things that had made me come to Rutherford, even with Jackson here. They let seniors begin to focus their coursework on what they wanted to major in instead of wasting our time. The majority of the classes I would be taking this year were English and literature related. I guess I could at least look forward to class, even if I dreaded everything else about this school.

I already had quite a bit of homework. This class in particular moved at a quick pace. I needed to have *To the Lighthouse* by Virginia Woolf done by next class period in two days.

Luckily, I'd already read it, thanks to Ms. Buckland, so I would just need to skim over it to prepare. I would hopefully have a chance at finishing the rest of my homework thanks to that.

"Are you going to the party tonight?" Lane asked as we headed to the cafeteria, where I was hopefully finally going to be able to eat something today.

"What party?" I asked, confused. Did everyone else not have the same amount of homework as I had?

"The football team always throws a rager at their frat the week before their first game. Almost all of the college students go, and most of the high school ones too for that matter, it's a mad house."

Football team meant Jackson. But it also meant that Melanie would most likely be gone, and I could get a lot of work done. I really needed to be smart here. Jackson had made it clear earlier that there was nothing but trouble to be had getting anywhere close to him.

I needed to heed that warning.

"I don't think so," I told her. "I really need to study."

"Booooo," said Lane, but it came across lighthearted.

"I just need to get my feet under me," I explained, and she gently nudged my shoulder.

"I'll let it slide just this once."

"Let me know how the party is," I told her as we stopped in front of my room.

"Of course. I'll be sure to say hi to Jackson for you."

I rolled my eyes as I opened the door and walked into a blissfully Melanie-free room.

THE DORMS WERE quiet that night. Much quieter than they had been the previous night. After getting all of my homework done for the next day's classes, I decided to take a shower. With everyone gone, it was unlikely that I would be in for a nasty surprise when I got back to my room, especially if I locked the door behind me.

Gathering my toiletries, I left the room, locking the door before proceeding to the showers.

Just as I suspected, it was a ghost town throughout the common area and the showers. I kind of hoped that there would be a party every night so that I could have this kind of silence.

I began to shower, humming a Taylor Swift song that had been playing on Spotify while I was studying. Suddenly, the door to the room opened, and then footsteps sounded as someone walked in.

Cursing the fact that someone had decided to not go to the party, I stopped humming and waited for the sound of their shower to start.

But there was nothing. There were no more footsteps, there was no shower...it was just silence.

Goosebumps crept up my spine. I didn't want to call out and sound like an idiot if someone was just primping in front of the mirror, but the silence was unnerving.

I finally heard footsteps again, but they didn't make me feel any better because they were walking towards the last shower stall...where I happened to be showering.

They stopped right in front of my shower, and I could see a pair of brown boots standing in front of my closed stall.

"I'm in here," I called out in a choked voice, feeling like I'd stepped into a horror film.

The person just continued to stand there, facing the stall, not making any other noises. My hands trembled as I reached for a towel...and that's when the person stood up on their tip toes and dropped a black snake over the top of the stall.

I screamed as the snake quickly recovered from its fall and winded its way towards me. I jumped up onto the shower bench, crying and trembling as the snake slithered around, not seeming to be bothered by the still running shower.

I hated snakes. *Loathed* them in fact. Snakes and the dark were enough to make me pee my pants in fear.

How was this actually happening?

The person took off just then, and I couldn't even follow them to see who it was, seeing as I was still trapped on the shower bench, paralyzed with fear. I heard the door to the room open and then close as the footsteps faded away.

The snake wasn't enormous, but it wasn't a tiny little garden snake either. What the fuck was someone doing with a snake in a dorm in the first place?

I stood there, trembling, as tears began to roll down my face, blending in with the water that was dripping from my sopping wet hair. Why would someone do that? And how was I going to get out of here?

How was I going to shower for the rest of the year?

The snake seemed to like my shower stall, not bothering to explore the rest of the expansive room. I knew I should just buck up and dart to the curtained off section where my things were and try to get out...the odds of the snake being poisonous were very slim. But I couldn't do that. So I stood there, fifteen minutes, then thirty minutes. Finally, the water went from hot to cold and I was a shivering, weeping mess.

The only good thing about that was that the snake seemed to not like the cold water so much and it finally began to slither away, trying to avoid the falling ice water. Once it slithered out of sight, I stood there for another ten minutes, just making sure that it wasn't lurking in the next stall, waiting to pounce as soon as I stepped off the bench.

Finally, I couldn't take the cold any longer, and I was going to have a nervous breakdown if I was in this room with that snake for a minute longer.

I jumped off the bench and threw my tiny, threadbare towel around me as I grabbed my things...still crying. I didn't care about the fact that whoever had thrown the snake could have tricked me and never left the room, I hadn't been paying that much attention due to the snake trying to come after me. I just needed out of there.

Luckily, the room was empty and the snake must have still been in the shower stalls as the main area by the sinks was snake-free as far as I could see. I ran to the door, my feet slipping and sliding due to the fact that I was still soaking wet.

The lounge area was still completely empty as I ran out

into it. Not that I thought the creepy voyeur was going to stick around if he or she wasn't still in the shower room waiting to jump me. I was frustrated because I wouldn't even be able to tell the school authorities what gender my creepy snake person was. The boots had been nondescript, a brown leather style that I'd seen on boys and girls.

I ran to my dorm room not caring if my lily-white ass was showing or not. I kept throwing looks behind me, making sure that the snake wasn't somehow following me.

In my panic, it took a minute for me to undo my door lock before I managed to get it open and get inside. Once in, I locked the door behind me and put my desk chair under the knob for good measure. Hopefully, Melanie would find someone she wanted to follow home tonight because I wasn't moving that chair.

Darting to my cell phone, I glanced at my bed and then threw off the top covers, sure there would be snakes lying in wait for me. When there was nothing...and my sheets were blissfully dry, I abandoned my plan to call school officials right away and went to work searching the room for any snakes or other creepy crawlies. Thirty minutes later, when I'd checked every one of the surprisingly numerous crevices in the room, I sank onto my bed, shivering and hiccupping as I came down from the adrenaline rush that only being trapped in a stall with a snake could bring.

Finally calming down, I grabbed my cell phone and looked up the dorm emergency number. When the person picked up, I frantically explained the situation, and they told me they would be right there.

I set my phone down, and then realized I was still in my tiny towel. I threw on some sweats and a tank and waited for the person to arrive.

Fifteen minutes later, there was a knock on my door.

Fifteen minutes seemed a little too long with the fact that there was an actual snake in the dorms, but what did I know?

Opening the door, there stood an annoyed looking man in a janitor's jumpsuit. "Were you the one who called about the snake?" he asked with a sigh, a look on his face like I had to be lying or I was drunk and seeing things.

"Yes," I answered, my voice coming out in a pathetic whimper. I cleared my throat. "It's in the shower rooms. Someone threw it in there while I was showering."

His eyes widened at that announcement. "Someone threw it at you while you were showering?" he clarified.

I nodded my head, tears threatening to spill just at the memory of it.

"Well...okay then. Let's go get this snake," he announced, backing away from the door and setting off towards the shower room.

I noticed that his hands were empty. "How are you going to catch the snake with your bare hands?" I called after him. He stopped and looked at his hands like he had just noticed.

"Right. I'll be back," he said, beginning to jog down the hallway towards the fire stairs.

Obviously, whoever I'd spoken with on the phone had thought that it was a prank and relayed that to the janitor.

I realized I was shivering, so I threw an old, holey sweatshirt over my tank top while I waited, my door closed and locked of course. I didn't like the sound of the janitor's use of the term "let's." If he thought I was following him into that room where the snake was waiting for me, he had another thing coming. The campus would be lucky if I ever showered again.

Five minutes later, there was a knock on my door, and I opened it to see the janitor standing there with what looked like a trash grabber and a bucket. I wasn't sure that either were going to be effective for this snake, but I guess he could try.

"Okay, I'm ready," he said, gesturing for me to move out of the safety of my room.

I took a few hesitant steps out into the hallway, wrapping my arms around myself. "It was in the last stall, and then it slithered away. Sorry...but I can't go in there with you. I may faint," I explained.

His eyes widened, and he took a step away from me like he was afraid my fainting might be catching. "That's alright. I'm sure I'll see it," he said as he continued to back away from me. I gave a sigh of relief as I watched him disappear into the shower room.

A minute later, he darted out, his face an ashen grey color as the shower door slammed behind him. "You weren't kidding," he said as he held the door closed behind him like the snake somehow had the ability to sprout arms and open the door and come after him.

I wouldn't put it past that snake actually.

"I'm going to call animal control," he stuttered, letting go of the door handle and darting away. I watched open mouthed as he ran to the stairs and disappeared from sight.

I slid back into my room, locked the door, and then crawled onto my bed. It was going to be a long night.

SCHOOL OFFICIALS WERE STILL INTERVIEWING me when drunken girls started to file back into the dorm, laughing and giggling as they stumbled to their rooms. They'd just missed the snake. I wonder how their drunken minds would have handled that sight.

Animal control had found it pretty quickly. It hadn't been poisonous—they assured me of that—but I'd caught a glimpse of it in the cage they'd brought as they carried it away and it seemed even bigger somehow.

Ms. Todd, the school official in charge of the dorm, grilled me on details of what had happened, and she seemed frustrated with me when I couldn't provide very many. "Is there anyone that would have an issue with you at this school?" she asked. "You did just start yesterday, did you not?"

I opened my mouth to say no, beyond the usual students who would hate me when they found out about my dad, but then I snapped it close as an image of Jackson's face darted through my mind.

The feet had definitely been too small for Jackson, but what if...

No. He wouldn't do that to me. Jackson had actually saved me from snakes when we were little. There would be no way that he would do something like that now, even with how much he seemed to hate me.

"I don't think so," I finally answered, feeling unsure for the first time about if I knew Jackson Parker at all. As it turned out, I hadn't really known his brother. Did the same thing apply to Jackson?

After Ms. Todd finally left, I locked the door once again, replaced the chair under the knob and crawled into bed. I left the lights blaring. I knew I wasn't going to sleep tonight.

Snakes.

Someone had it out for me. And I just hoped it wasn't *him*.

Only News, Never Opinions.　　　　　　　　　　　　　　　12 august

Dayton Valley News

Your Best Source of News Since 1965

High School Football Star Still in Critical Condition. Mystery Surrounding Injuries.

Caiden Parker, South High's Star Tight End is still said to be in critical condition after an August 11th car accident. His companion in the vehicle, fellow high-school student Everly James is also in critical condition. Parker received a traumatic brain injury however a source has stated that some of Parker's injuries appear to be unrelated to the accident itself. Hospital administrators have refused to comment. Parker was driving in a vehicle with fellow classmate, Everly James. James sustained a traumatic brain injury, a broken femur, a broken arm, a ruptured spleen, and punctured lungs. James left surgery yesterday and is said to be stabilized in the ICU. Parker is is known with his twin brother, Jackson an -
Story Continued on A5.

7

THEN

It had been a long time since I'd had a birthday party. I remembered when I was little, my father would throw lavish parties to show off all our wealth. One time, I had a whole fucking petting zoo set up on the front lawn of our mansion.

But that was *before*.

Since the year my father put a bullet in his brain, I'd never had another party. In fact, my mother had gone out of her way to ignore it. Like somehow my birth, instead of her and my father's greed had been the precipice in bringing about our family's downfall.

Once the twins had come into my life, there had been private celebrations that always included my favorite chocolate chip cupcake from the local bakery and a solitary candle that I blew out at midnight, but there had never been a party. Especially like this.

The twin's sixteenth birthday party. They'd been talking about plans for it for months, but it was one thing to hear about it and another to see it.

I looked through the gate at the chaos that had already started. I'd just ridden my bike to the party. Jackson and Caiden had offered to come pick me up, but I'd lied and told them my mom could give me a ride, not wanting them to be inconvenienced with me on the day of their party.

But now I wished I'd accepted their offer, since the bike ride had left me a sweaty mess. School would be out soon, and summer was already trying to rear its head. I slipped through the gate that led into the massive few acres of property that made up the twin's backyard and used my key to slink my way into the pool house to try and make myself less like a pile of melted ice cream.

I fidgeted with the red bikini that I'd found at the thrift shop the other day. I'd heard people say that it was gross to wear someone else's bathing suit, but I'd figured the two times I'd sent it through the wash had gotten rid of any germs in it. And besides, it looked really good on me. I'd finally started to get some curves over the school year, and my flat chest had settled into a B cup. My hips and ass had started to come in as well...which meant that my clothes no longer fit. When I'd asked for more clothes for school, my mom had just told me that I was getting fat and I should get on a diet because she wouldn't be getting me new clothes. Since I didn't have any money, the fact that my curves had come in had been really noticeable this year, since all my clothes were skintight.

Well, noticeable to everyone but *them*.

Taking a deep breath, I threw on my simple black cover-up and stuffed the rest of my sweaty clothes in the corner of the room. Then I stepped back out of the pool house, making sure to lock the room behind me. The twins wanted their main hangout area in the pool house to stay locked and for everyone to use the main pool house bathroom that had an entrance on the other side. I was the only person they trusted with a key, and even after all these years of being best friends with them, it still made me feel special.

I tried to hold my head up high as I stepped into the sights of the other partygoers. The twin's pool was massive with several slides, two hot tubs, and a full on rock grotto. Pool chairs were set up everywhere, and almost all of them were filled already. A massive slip and slide was set up on the hill behind the pool, and there was even a DJ cranking out tunes on the other side of the pool. Several tables were set up with catered food featuring all of the twin's favorites, and judging by all the people carrying around red solo cups, I was sure there was alcohol around here somewhere.

I looked around surreptitiously for the twins, trying not to look like I cared about all the stares I was getting. I was tolerated at this point. Everyone knew better than to call me anything in front of the guys. But I was a sitting duck right now without them around.

A throaty laugh caught my attention, and I caught sight of Veronica Hollingsworth trying to wrap herself around Jackson. He was ignoring her as he talked to Caiden and one of the other football players, but it was still hard to see her touching him. I'd heard the rumors. Jackson Parker got around, and Veronica was one of his frequent playmates.

Caiden had his own set of groupies who hung on his every word, but I caught his eye as I stood there awkwardly, and he immediately ditched them to jog over to me. His sunny smile almost took my breath away. They'd always been good-looking. But when you were a little kid, you cared more if someone was nice to you than what they looked like. He and Jackson had both gotten so hot that sometimes I couldn't look right at them. I had to focus on one characteristic on their face so that I didn't get overwhelmed and could carry on a normal conversation with them.

"LyLy, my girl," he said, immediately pressing a kiss to the side of my head, and he gave me a hug. My heart raced being up against him. He pressed his six-pack against my arm, and it should have been fucking illegal for a sixteen-year-old to have that good of a body. Between his dark hair, his tan skin, and his yellow swim trunks that were hanging dangerously low, I was in danger of passing out.

I tried not to make it super obvious how worked up I was when I gently pushed away from him.

"Happy birthday," I said softly, looking up at the face I had memorized. Both the twins were already pushing six foot three, towering over my measly five foot six form and it was just another thing about them that made me feel protected.

"You're late," he commented, gesturing to the craziness around me. Three members of the football team had just thrown in some of the popular girls and they were pretending to shriek at the water temperature, even though the twins kept the pool at a perfect eighty degrees year-round.

"I noticed," I commented, looking around as well. My gaze got caught on Jackson's, suddenly. He was still on the other side of the pool, Veronica wrapped around him, half the football team trying to get his attention. The sight of him, so intent and staring right at me, pushed all the air out of my lungs.

"Jackson's holding court," Caiden commented sarcastically, even though he'd been doing the same thing before he saw me. Popularity was effortless for the twins, even if they had me bringing them down.

I pried my eyes away from Jackson's, unable to deal with the way that he stared at me.

"Let's go swimming," urged Caiden, swooping me into his arms and pretending to run towards the pool. I shrieked, the same way I'd just been mocking those other girls for doing. He stopped right at the edge and gave me a dark smile. "Want to take your cover-up off first?" he asked, and I nodded shyly, my heart beating out of rhythm at the thought of showing so much skin in front of half the school.

"You're safe for now," he said with a laugh, setting me down. "Move," he ordered a guy from my class, Trevor I think was his name, who happened to be set up on a pool chair nearest to where we were standing.

I snorted when Trevor immediately got up like someone had lit a fire underneath him, and Trevor shot me a dirty look as he passed by me. I walked over to the chair, took a deep breath, and then tore off my safety net. I heard a small intake of breath behind me, but when I whirled around to look at where it had come from, it was just Caiden standing there with a blank face. For a moment, I thought I caught sparks of hunger in his eyes as he traced the shape of my body from head to toe, but whatever the look was, it was gone in a moment.

"Pool time," grinned Caiden. And before I could blink, he'd grabbed me and jumped into the pool with me in his arms. I sputtered as I swallowed some water. The near drowning wasn't enough to distract me from the fact that Caiden's right hand had just stroked my side, perilously close to my right boob. He lingered there for a second, and I temporarily forgot to breathe. After what seemed like an hour, but was probably only a minute, he wrapped both arms around me again and set his chin on top of my head. I looked up and caught Jackson staring at me again.

I knew he'd look at me again, and I'd prepared myself for the racing heart and ragged breathing. I was ready for one of his signature winks that he'd always given me, and for the flames that would burn up my cheeks as they always did when our gazes locked lately.

But I didn't know it would hurt.

I couldn't plan ahead for the ache that lived in my chest when he didn't acknowledge my wave. I hadn't thought to be thankful for an empty stomach, courtesy of my mother drinking away our grocery budget this month, until it flipped when his gaze flicked to Caiden wrapped around me. His jaw clenched as tight as the fists by his sides.

I didn't know how empty I'd feel when he glared at my lips and my mouthed hello, but then ignored it and turned back to his conversation with his team, this time making sure to add Veronica to the mix.

Okay... I almost got hit by a volleyball that had just been tossed over the net set up in the middle of the pool as that one minute with me here and Jackson all the way over there rolled on replay. I wasn't sure what I'd done, or what had changed since I spoke to him on the phone the night before, other than everything. I hide my hurt by pretending to play volleyball with Caiden and berated myself for the absurdity of it. I should be used to Jackson's moods by now. Except Jackson had never ignored me.

THE REST of the day passed similarly, and I was ready to leave early, even though I'd been anticipating this day for months. Caiden got me some of the alcoholic punch that had been making the rounds, and I sipped it as I watched Jackson out of the corner of my eye. Caiden had wrapped himself around me all day. Even now, when he was talking to some of his friends, his arm was casually draped around my waist. The twins had always been touchy-feely, but I wasn't quite sure what to make of how either of them were acting today.

The sun had started to set before the twin's staff brought out an enormous three-tiered cake. I sang along with everyone else as they basked in the attention of their adoring classmates. Jackson even managed to crack a rare smile as they both blew out the sixteen candles in tandem. Booze was immediately brought out, and the DJ changed the songs from the sun-soaked playlist that had been blasting all day to songs that would better fit a club.

Caiden looked around, probably to drag me on the dance floor, but I slipped away before he spotted me, running to hide in the locked pool house bedroom where no one would be able to find me.

Sometimes, crowds could get...overwhelming for me. Caiden could never understand that. He lived for the limelight. Jackson and I were alike that way though. Although Jackson was popular, he could only handle small doses of crowds before he started to get twitchy. And when he started to descend into one of his depressive episodes...then he really hated crowds. The only time Caiden and Jackson were alike socially was when Jackson was in his "black" moods. Then Jackson was up for anything.

I called it black because Jackson was one of the rare cases where his actual eye color changed if he was becoming manic. It had become a habit of mine over the years to always look at eyes to assess his moods.

I didn't know why I thought about that now.

Maybe I was trying to blame how he'd treated me all day on an impending episode. That would probably make me feel better.

I sank into one of the squishy armchairs in the room and sighed as I pulled out my phone to start reading. I could readily admit at that moment how socially awkward I sometimes was.

Just then, the handle on the door started moving and a key turned in the lock. A second later, Jackson came in.

He hadn't seen me—my chair was hidden in the corner behind a plant on the wall behind the door. He closed the door and leaned against it, not bothering to look around the room. He scrubbed his hands over his face and sighed. "Fuck," he muttered.

For some reason, I didn't want to announce my presence. It was rare that I got to observe Jackson in such a way. He always had his walls up. Being bipolar only made him more disciplined, afraid to ever let go since he didn't have much control over himself during his "black" episodes.

He pulled out his phone, and his thumb hovered on my contact information. After a second of indecision, he started typing out a text. I quickly silenced my phone. At this point, I felt like an idiot that I hadn't announced myself, and I wasn't going to do it now.

A few seconds later, a text came through my phone.

Where are you?

I didn't answer, not knowing what to say, at least right now. I'd gladly answer when he was out of here and I didn't stand the chance of looking like the biggest idiot in the world.

He stood there for a long moment, waiting for my answer. When I didn't send one, he cursed again and then opened the door and went back outside. I sank back in my chair, adrenaline coursing through me over what had just happened. What was his problem tonight? What was my problem tonight?

After giving Jackson a five-minute head start, so I at least stood the chance of him not seeing me, I went back outside to the party that had morphed into a rager while I'd been inside. I locked the door behind me, took a deep breath, and stepped out from behind the palm trees that shielded the entrance.

I found Caiden right away, dancing in a big group. He looked around the dance floor every couple of minutes, and I knew he was looking for me. I stayed in the shadows so he wouldn't see me, not really understanding why I wanted to hide from him. I looked around for Jackson, but he was nowhere in sight.

Suddenly, a familiar set of hands gripped my waist, and I was tugged back against Jackson's chest.

I basked for an instant in his embrace; the heat radiating from him to me fracturing my heart into scattered palpitations. A low rumble vibrated between us as his fingers dug into my hips. "Where were you hiding, little angel?"

His breath was rough—it was, I felt it—but then he pushed me gently away. It seemed like I had imagined it when I turned to find he was raking his hand through his hair from root to tip, jaw tense.

"I just needed a break," I whispered, my voice coming out low and throaty from whatever this was between us right now.

He looked me over, getting stuck on my lips and then my hair. His gaze landed on my eyes, and a struggle rolled around in his blue storm. But he shook his head as if to free himself from confusion.

"Want to dance?" he asked, a wicked glint in his eye as he stretched out his hand towards me. I hesitated for a moment. Danger lingered in his question.

And then, like always when it came to Jackson Parker, I leaped.

I took his outstretched hand and stared at our connection. His grip was warm, firm, and electric, very much like his eyes that drew me in. He led me to the dance floor, and it said a lot for the spell I was under that I was only faintly aware of the gazes tracking our every move.

"Jackson," called out Caiden, who had just spotted us. He motioned for us to join him, but Jackson waved him away and pulled me close to him.

The song changed just then to "Past Life" by Trevor Daniel and I sank into Jackson's embrace. The music twirled like thread around us. I rested my head against his chest, and let him lead me in a wicked, slow dance that didn't match the tempo of the song at all. Closing my eyes, I soaked in the feel of him.

The song ended, and I opened my eyes, only to realize that Jackson had maneuvered us away from the crowd again. We were on the edge of the dance floor. We continued to move slowly as the song switched to "One Thing Right" by Marshmello.

He stopped suddenly and stared at me with those fathomless blue eyes. I could've sworn in that moment that the whole universe was reflected in those depths.

"Everly," he breathed into the silence, my name a prayer on his lips. His eyes slowly started to close, and then he leaned in, so his mouth hovered over mine, not touching, just taking. It was so intimate. More intimate than anything I'd ever experienced in my life. But I wanted to kiss him.

"Jackson," I whispered, and the word broke the spell.

When his eyes opened, a devilish gleam replaced the adoration that had been in his gaze before. He smiled, a slow, beguiling grin, as I writhed against his dark stare and the attention he gave me.

"Do you want this, little angel? Tell me you need this as much as I do." I was speechless as he leaned forward and pressed the barest hint of a kiss against my lips. I'd only been kissed once before, by his brother, in fact. It was a kiss done under the bleachers that we never spoke of again.

But this...

This was a kiss.

Every kiss in my life had been practice for this one, and each kiss thereafter would have this one to live up to. I sank deeply and desperately into his arms, lost in the unfamiliarity of being found.

"Yes," I barely breathed out before his head dipped and his lips pressed against me again, but more firmly this time. My mouth opened on a gasp, and he slid the tip of his tongue against me. My body arched against him at the sweet, carnal sensation, and I let out a soft moan. Closing my eyes, I focused on him, and the tormenting flicks of his tongue.

Wrapping his arms around me, he became impassioned, groaning as he lifted me up against him so that I fit perfectly in his embrace. I couldn't move, my only outlet the soft sighs falling almost soundlessly into the still air. I surrendered to the beautiful intensity, panting.

His lips left mine briefly, giving me a chance to suck in

oxygen since I seemed to have forgotten how to breathe correctly in the wake of his life-changing kiss.

"Jackson," I pleaded. His lips met mine again in response. We began to move as the song switched again. But the real music was his mouth, playing artfully against mine. He looked down at me, eyes scorching and erotic, his mouth and tongue insistent and hot as he teased me. The longing and desire built between us, his mouth taking me higher and higher. I writhed against him, the dance becoming feverish. I needed, I wanted.

I was still dressed in just my bathing suit, and he slid his finger past my bikini bottoms, inside my welcoming body. "Is this okay?" he breathed desperately.

Two fingers plunged into me once, twice, his tongue flicked and rolled against mine, and he launched me into something I hadn't expected, something that I'd never experienced before. I exploded, and he caught my scream against his mouth. Waves of pleasure crashed through my entire body, and I bowed against him once more. His fingers continued moving on me, in me, pushing my orgasm on and on.

When I couldn't stand it anymore, I tugged his hair, and he gently slid his fingers out of me. Diving into his mouth, I relished the feel of his lips as they continued to stroke over mine. Without thought, I grabbed his bottom lip between my teeth, sucking on it. I drank in his low moan, and spurred him on for more.

"Jackson?" His name was a question on my lips because I didn't know what just happened between us. Our gazes met, his a stunning blue, mine bewildered by the staggering amount of emotion coursing through me for my best friend. The boy who had been my protector, my confidant, my hero...but never my lover. My thoughts scattered, frayed with unbridled tension, and I dissolved against him, mind and body desperate to surrender to this mystifying connection between us.

"Jackson!" someone called out. And just like that the spell was shattered, broken, breaking off in the breeze as it surrounded us.

"Shit," he muttered as he stared at me desperately. "Everly... I—" he began. And then Caiden appeared. He stopped in his tracks when he noticed how close our faces were to each other.

"Hey guys," he said slowly, but there was an edge of anger to his voice that sent guilt spiraling through me. For what reason...I wasn't sure.

"Jackson, get over here," he said, his voice forced. "Are my two people going to leave me to celebrate alone?"

Jackson lifted an eyebrow at his brother's dramatics, seeming to be unperturbed at the position his brother had found us in. "The five hundred people at this party count as you celebrating alone?"

Caiden's tense mood evaporated, and he reached out and pulled both of us towards him, clapping us both on the back before he dragged us back towards the center of the dance floor where a raucous cheer rose up at the return of the twins.

I danced, but it was like I was in a trance.

Jackson Parker had kissed me.

He had kissed me.

I had kissed him.

What was going to happen now?

Jackson, for his part, didn't seem to be having the same conflicted thoughts as I was. He danced around like he was Justin Timberlake, he and Caiden engaging in some dance-offs that had everyone cheering.

He never made eye contact with me once.

And at the end of the night, when I slunk into the pool house because I was too tired and too tipsy to even think about going home, it was between both boys that I laid my head.

8

NOW

Jackson

It would be easy to destroy her, because I knew her.

I knew all the dark thoughts she kept in that pretty little head of hers. I knew what made her tick, what made her smile...what made her cry. It was interesting really, how one person could call to both the best and worst parts of you. Before everything had happened, I'd lived for the sight of her smile. I'd spent years plotting how I could make her happy, how I could be enough for her, how I could be everything for her.

Little did I know, she'd spent years plotting, too.

I wouldn't make the same mistakes now that I had then — "Are you even paying attention to anything I'm saying?" Charise asked crossly.

She'd been trying to do some kind of sexy dance that consisted of a lot of grinding on my dick.

"Sorry, doll, proceed," I told her, shooting her a cocky grin that had her immediately melting against me.

Simon guffawed next to me at the fact that I'd somehow managed to daydream while a hot chick was throwing herself at me. I said guffawed, because my outside linebacker teammate had a laugh that could level whole forests. I shot him a glare to get him to shut up. I didn't want to be reminded why I'd been distracted.

Charise was an attractive girl. I'd give her that. Just my type with her black hair, and her fake boobs, and a mouth that was like a fucking Hoover. I'd banged her the week before in the locker room, and she'd been creaming for another round ever since then. She'd been a good fuck, but she screamed grade A clinger.

That was why my dick just wasn't interested tonight.

Or at least, that was what I was telling myself.

"You got Landry pretty fucking good, my man," commented Tommy, one of the wide receivers on the team and the closest person to a best friend that I had at this school.

I smirked as I looked over to where the hockey team was holding court after their win that evening. Landry shot daggers at me from across the room, and I gave him the finger. Fucking prick.

I'd never had a particular problem with Landry. We mostly stayed out of each other's way, occasionally saying hello when we were both at the same party.

Today...that definitely changed. He'd just been lucky I hadn't been manic today or I would've given him more than a black eye.

I didn't want to examine too closely why that was — okay, I knew exactly why that was. I'd lost my fucking mind when I saw him talking to Everly.

Everly. Fuck. I closed my eyes and tried to control my dick as I thought about her. There was a reason that I'd only fucked girls who weren't blondes for the last few years.

She had ruined me for all blondes.

"There's a room open upstairs," came a whisper in my ear, and my eyes popped open to see Charise an inch away from devouring my lips. Fucking hell. I needed to get out of here.

I leaned away from her, and she gave me a confused look. I could see how my achingly hard dick could be giving her the wrong signals.

"I've got to get out of here," I told her, pushing her away gently and standing up. Her gaze greedily took in the sliver of skin peeking out from under my shirt. Shit, she was worse than a guy in front of a pair of perfect tits.

Speaking of perfect tits... Everly's...

I grabbed Charise and pulled her towards me, attacking her lips like I was desperate.

Nope, still wasn't helping. I pulled back, swearing.

Charise looked like she was going to faint. Faint or try and roofie me so she could jump my dick and have my babies.

"See you around," I told her with a smile that I hoped would distract her for a minute before she realized how fucked up what had just happened was. I gave a sarcastic salute to Simon and Tommy, who were both looking at me like I'd lost my mind, and then I left before Charise could come out of the trance my kiss had thrown her in and follow me home.

The party had been on Frat Row, and I lived off-campus with Simon and Tommy, but I found myself walking towards the dorm where Everly was living. It was late, but all the lights were on, and I watched as some of the school staff walked up the steps.

I grinned and took a deep breath.

Yep, it was going to be easy to destroy her...because I knew her.

&

Everly

"Fucking snakes," Lane griped the next morning as we grabbed breakfast, shivering as I told her what had happened. "Who do you think did it?" she asked as I tried to decide between a Belgian waffle or an egg white omelet.

Hell, was it even a decision? I grabbed the waffle, smothered it with syrup, and then put a big scoop of cream on top of it for good measure. "No idea," I lied, or at least, I think I lied. Jackson's face was starring front and center in my mind, but I couldn't be sure. At least not yet. It could have still been Melanie, who'd dared to bring a guy to our room at four in the morning. I'd just gone to sleep an hour before, and her beating on the door when it wasn't unlocked had almost given me a heart attack. My determination to get along with my new roommate had flown out the window, and I'd told her she wasn't allowed in unless the asshole with her left.

Needless to say, we weren't on speaking terms this morning.

I was really going to need to find a way to get a new room assignment before Melanie smothered me in my sleep.

We sat down at an empty table to eat. The group of girls seated at the table next to us gave us ugly looks, like we'd just brought the plague to their side of the room.

"It's kind of terrifying that someone at this school is

throwing snakes at people," Lane said uneasily, looking around the room suspiciously.

I shivered at the memory of the snake slithering closer to me, and I looked around the room too, even though I knew I was only looking for one person in particular.

He wouldn't do something like that to me, I swore to myself. But then again, the last time I'd talked to him two years before, there had been utter blankness in his gaze as he'd stared at me like I was nothing.

I'd never thought he could look at me like that either.

I pursed my lips and pushed my plate of waffles away from me, my appetite disappearing.

Lane continued to eat and people watch, and I stared at her hard, suddenly suspicious.

"Why are you being so nice to me?" I asked, eyeing her critically. "Surely your job as my student liaison is complete now that I've been here a few days."

She smirked at me and finished chewing before she answered. "I don't know how you could have missed it, but I'm not exactly Ms. Popular around here. I'm not going to run from the chance to actually be friends with someone who doesn't have a fuck ton of preconceived notions about me or the strong belief that primary colors don't belong in someone's hair." She sighed. "It's nice to have a friend." There's an air of vulnerability about her in that moment, and it called to me.

I was pretty sure my soul decided at that moment that we were going to be sisters. Damage called to damage and all of that.

Just then, Jackson walked in the room, surrounded by an entourage of girls and guys all desperate to get his attention. I swore all the air in the room got swallowed up.

My reaction was utterly ridiculous. How was it that for

two years I'd been immune to desire, and at the mere sight of this gorgeous, completely out-of-everyone's-league man, I was salivating like a bitch in heat? My reaction to Jackson had always been completely insane.

I stared at him like I was obsessed, and hell, maybe I was. Lane turned to see what I was so entranced with and snorted when she saw that it was Jackson.

"Do I need to start giving you five reasons why you should stay away from him every time he's in the vicinity?" she snarked.

"Maybe," I muttered, distracted, as I continued to stare avidly at Jackson.

It was like he could feel me looking at him, because his eyes caught mine from across the room. Maybe it was my imagination, but it almost looked like his steps faltered for a moment.

It was his turn to stare. His intense gaze held mine for what felt like an eternity. His eyes continued with their hypnotic spell as his cohort invaded the moment, hurling questions and ideas at him as they tried to get his attention.

I couldn't stand his stare after a while. The room felt like it was going to boil over around me. I stood, and my hands fanned over the brown leather mini skirt I'd found at a thrift store to make sure it was lying smoothly over my rounded hips. I licked my lip, a habit that I'd never been able to break when I was nervous, and his gaze tripped over the area I'd just caressed.

When he finally looked away, I should have been relieved, but instead I felt lost.

Lane dragged me out of the room before I did something crazy like try and talk to him.

"What's your deal with him? Did you meet him before

coming here? Because Eves...he's hot as fuck. But you look at him like you're literally dying."

I smiled bitterly as I tried to get ahold of myself now that we were out of his presence. "We were childhood friends," I admitted. "And now we're not."

She seemed to get that I wasn't going to say anything more on the subject, because she quickly started a snarky explanation of all the frats on campus and why they all sucked.

I nodded along, listening avidly as we walked to my next class.

I realized when we were almost there that I'd forgotten the book that the professor had emailed us was mandatory for class. I had practically every other school book in the bag on my back. But somehow, I was missing that one. "Ugh," I moaned, knowing that my limp was going to make me late. "I forgot the book I need back in my room. I've got to go get it."

Lane hesitated, clearly torn between not wanting to be late for class and not wanting to make me walk alone.

"Go to class," I told her as I started to walk off. "Meet for dinner?" I called out shyly when I was a few steps away, the question making me feel nervous.

"For sure!" she responded excitedly before rushing to the building where her class was located.

I hustled back to my thankfully Melanie-free room to grab my book. I ran a hand over my sheets as I walked by...just in case.

Thankfully they were dry.

I was five minutes late when I finally got back to the building where my class was. Rutherford had three sets of different classes Monday through Wednesday, with Wednesday's classes being the only classes that were only once a week. Monday and Tuesday's set of classes had been Jackson-free, but as soon as I walked into the room for this one, Creative Writing, I knew my luck had run out.

It was literally everything I could do to prevent myself from looking around the room to locate him.

"Oh, there you are. I was beginning to think you'd dropped out of the class due to my brutal reputation," joked the professor, a man who was way too young looking and way too attractive to be a professor at this school.

I forgot how to make words for a minute at the sight of his vibrant hazel eyes peeking out from a mess of inky black hair. I was pretty sure there was a tattoo peeking out from the top of his sweater as well.

The smile he was giving me suggested that he knew exactly what I was thinking, and he cleared his throat to pull me back to the present.

"You're Ms. James, right?" he clarified, and I nodded, still a bit tongue-tied.

"Everly," I squeaked, and I heard a few snorts from some of the class.

The professor, Professor Brady, I now remembered was his name, looked around the room. "It looks like there's an empty desk by Mr. Parker," he commented, and I froze in place, ready to bolt.

I shook myself out of it though, remembering all the reviews that I'd read on the school portal online about how amazing this class was. I'd had to submit a writing sample to even be accepted, and I was the only senior in the class. All the rest were from the college.

Jackson Parker wasn't going to take this away from me.

I had to finally look to see where he was sitting so that I could take my seat. Although I already knew, I could feel his eyes beating into me as soon as I'd stepped into the classroom.

He was sitting towards the back. I was sure the only reason there was an empty desk next to him was because everyone was afraid to sit there unless they were invited to. His features were carefully blank as I walked towards my desk, but his eyes were wild.

I sat down, careful to keep my body as far away from him as possible.

"Alright, now that we're all here, I'm not going to waste my time in giving you a long overview of the class. You have the syllabus, and you're not five years old. We're going to get right into it. This first assignment will help me see where you're at. I've seen writing samples from all of you, but I want to see how you do on the spot. Today, you're going to spend the next hour writing about your first kiss. If you haven't been kissed yet, we'll get you signed up for Tinder, and then you can write about what you want your first kiss to be like." The class tittered at his joke, and he smirked. Professor Brady's gaze met mine briefly, an interested spark in their depths that was hard to interpret. But I wasn't one of the amused students.

I don't think that he could have asked me to write about something worse. I would have rather written about my dad blowing his brains out than this subject.

Caiden had been my first kiss.

I peeked over at Jackson. He gripped the desk in front of him so hard that his knuckles had turned white.

I felt like throwing up, and I was actually grateful that I'd only had a few bites of my waffle.

"Better get started, Everly," Jackson whispered harshly to me, and I cringed.

Torture would be preferable to the next hour we would

spend writing as I was forced to relive the moment I'd planted a seed that would later destroy my best friends.

"Jackson kissed Marcy Thomas," Caiden told me in the hallway, rolling his eyes. "The idiot." I was twelve and the twins were thirteen, and while I knew that the girls at our school eyed them both like they were their favorite flavor of candy, the idea of Jackson actually kissing one of them was so foreign, it took me a moment to wrap my head around it.

"Are you sure?" I asked, and I was ashamed because I knew my lip was quivering.

Caiden studied me, a small frown on his face. He opened his mouth to say something, but the bell chose to ring at that moment. "Meet me after class by the football bleachers before practice starts, Ly Ly," he said, then made me promise as he walked backward away from me. I agreed, of course, because I always agreed to whatever they wanted. But all I could think about was Jackson and the fact that it felt like I'd been stabbed in the heart.

Jackson texted me during class, but I ignored it, not ready to admit to myself why. My heart was still in my throat when the class ended, and I had no idea what the teacher had even said. I hurried outside, wanting to feel Caiden's sunshine to get me out of the mood I was in. He was texting someone when I got there, but he immediately pocketed his phone when he saw me. Caiden's smile lit up his whole face, and it was as if something settled inside of me.

"Hi," I said lamely, and he laughed and pulled me into his arms for a hug. Instead of letting me go afterward, he continued to hold me close.

"You've never been kissed, have you, Ly Ly?" he asked, a wicked grin on his too handsome face.

I shook my head, the question making me too shy to answer.

"You know, I could give you your first one. There's no use waiting around anymore, is there?"

I looked up at him, my cheeks flushing. He knew about my crush on Jackson?

"What do you say, Everly? Can I give you your first kiss?" Caiden asked as he lowered his lips to mine.

A nervous fluttering lit up my insides...along with a sense of wrongness that I shook off. This was my best friend. And it was just a kiss. And as I thought about the fact that Jackson had given his kiss away, I closed my eyes and leaned in as Caiden's lips met mine.

It was just one sweet kiss. There was only a slip of tongue even. But Caiden looked oddly triumphant as I pulled away from him. "Love you, Ly Ly," he told me like he always did.

It was just one kiss...

"Time's up," Professor Brady announced, and my hands oddly trembled as they pulled away from the keyboard.

"Go ahead and email them to me, and I'll look them over the next few days. There will be a sign-up sheet sent out this weekend for office hours Monday and Tuesday to discuss your writing. Have a good rest of the week!" he called out as a bell rang, and we all started to gather our things.

I got my stuff together like the room was on fire. I didn't dare look at Jackson, not breathing until I'd made my way out of the building and was safely ensconced on a bench hidden by a tree a few buildings down. I still had one class to go to, but I was shaking and needed a second to recover.

I still wasn't recovered when I settled into my bed that night.

A loud banging on the door had me bolting upright, my heart beating a million miles a minute.

"Who the fuck is that?" groaned Melanie as she pulled her pillow over her head. I'd been sleeping with one eye open the whole night since she was in the room tonight, and the rude awakening was not welcome.

"Everrrrrrrly," Jackson called through the door, and I didn't know it was possible, but my heart started racing even faster, until I was sure that I was going to have a heart attack.

"Open up," he sang. He was drunk.

The old Jackson was never drunk. He loathed losing control too much to have more than a few beers at a time.

He sounded trashed right now. I glanced at my phone, it was two in the morning.

I hurried to the door and opened it just a few inches.

"Little angel, let me in," he whispered loudly and my traitorous heart clenched at the nickname I hadn't heard since before the accident.

"Jackson, it's two in the morning," I said before reluctantly opening the door and letting him in.

"Is that Jackson Parker?" Melanie almost squealed as she sat up in bed looking far more alert than she had a second earlier. She immediately started to run her fingers through her hair like she had a chance of impressing him. I growled internally at the thought.

"Out, Loose Lips," he snarled drunkenly at her as soon as he noticed her, and she gasped, affronted. The derogatory way he said it made me think that he wasn't talking about the lips on her face when he called her that.

"Fuck you, Parker," she said halfheartedly, since we all knew she would fuck him in an instant if she could. She grabbed a sweatshirt and pulled it over her as she darted past us. Melanie gave me an appraising look as she walked out, a look that spelled trouble for me. She pounded on the door two doors down, and a girl I'd seen her walking with sleepily opened the door and let her in.

"That wasn't nice, Jackson," I said quietly as he walked in and immediately made himself at home on my bed. He had an adorable look on his face as he sighed against my pillow. I closed the door and locked it behind me before staring again at the intruder who'd taken over my bed.

"Come here, little angel," he said seductively as he moved over to give me space on the bed.

Yes, he was drunk. Maybe drunk wasn't the right word. Wasted was probably a more apt description. But I couldn't stop myself from getting into that bed with him.

It was like a missing piece of myself slid into place as he pulled my back towards his chest and wrapped his arms around me. His chin fit perfectly tucked against the top of my head, and I had to take a deep breath to ward off the tears that were threatening from the familiar move.

"Why are you here, Jackson?" I finally asked quietly, and he groaned.

"Have you been thinking about that kiss since class too?" he slurred. And my heart stuttered.

"What kiss?" I pressed him, a terrible suspicion coming over me.

"When I kissed you at my birthday party. Your first kiss. It was the best kiss," he commented in a singsong voice.

Fuck, my heart hurt. Had he really thought this whole time that he'd been my first kiss?

"Tell me it was the best kiss, Everly," he ordered as his voice shifted into an almost dream-like state. His hands caressed my throat, and it was like I'd forgotten how to breathe.

"It was the best kiss, Jackson," I answered softly.

But he was already snoring. So he couldn't hear how badly he had broken my heart once again.

In a better world, he would have been my first kiss.

In a better world, I would have answered that text of his and never met Caiden under the bleachers.

In my dreams, that kiss at his sixteenth birthday party had been my first kiss.

I fell into a deep sleep despite my best efforts to stay awake.

And when I woke up, Jackson was gone.

And I'd never felt more alone.

9

THEN

It was never a good omen when there was a full moon and Friday the thirteenth all in the same week. I blamed that for the unease that was trickling down my spine as I walked out to the car where the twins waited for me. Now that they were sixteen and could drive, we were all looking forward to our first summer of them not having to convince their parents to pick me up when we wanted to hang out, or me having to take a bus, ride my bike, or walk to get to wherever they were.

They both were spoiled brats and had been given brand new cars for the day after their birthday party. Jackson had picked a black, lifted F150 while Caiden had chosen a yellow Jeep.

I'd snorted when I'd seen their cars. They couldn't have more stereotypically described them if they tried.

Jackson had already warned me that they were going to take turns picking me up during the summer because they both wanted to drive their cars. But today, they had both ridden in Jackson's truck for the beginning of our last week of school. They both knew how hard the end of the school year always was for me.

As much as I hated school and the continuous taunting I experienced there, at least it meant I spent all day away from my mother. The end of school also meant that we would be a few months closer to me being alone at school. Next year, the twins would be attending their junior year at Rutherford Academy, an exclusive school that only had junior and senior grades in the high school portion of the school, so even though I'd been admitted as well on scholarship, I couldn't attend until the next year. It felt like complete bullshit that the twin's May birthday had allowed them to be a whole grade ahead of my September birthday, but maybe that was my fear talking. After so many years with them by my side, I wasn't sure how I was going to handle next year.

The twin's parents, however, were probably relieved we were done attending the same school for at least a year. Jackson and Caiden had both been sent to the principal's office a dozen times at least this year, trying to defend me from the crap that our classmates continued to throw my way.

You would think after years of being called every name in the book, some of them exceptionally original might I add, that I would have been numb to it before now. Unfortunately, that hadn't been the case, and the guys weren't willing to let me just try and ignore it.

I had a lot of toughening up to do this summer.

"There's my girl," said Caiden as he hopped out and opened the door for me. Before I could get in, he pulled me into his arms and wrapped me in a tight hug. I savored it, breathing in the spicy bergamot and citrus scent of his cologne. Caiden reached inside the front seat and handed me the mocha latte they'd picked up for me, and I grinned at him, immediately taking a sip of the chocolatey goodness.

I hopped in the back seat and caught Jackson's sunglasses-covered stare in the rearview mirror. "Hey, Eves," he said with a slow smile that belied the intensity I could feel, even without being able to see his actual eyes. Something...was happening between us. Something I couldn't quite describe. Ever since the twin's birthday party two weeks earlier...

Caiden started to chatter about something as Jackson and I continued to stare at each other.

"Guys?" Caiden asked with a frown when Jackson still hadn't made a move to head to school. He noticed what Jackson's attention was caught on, and his frown deepened. "We're going to be late," he growled, a reaction that caught both of our attention. Caiden didn't growl.

Jackson cleared his throat and shot his brother a look, but chose not to say anything. The truck was weirdly silent for the rest of the drive, a strange tension threaded between the three of us.

We parked, and Caiden got out of the truck and rushed to open the door for me, still sulking for some reason.

"You okay?" I asked softly, hating when either of them was mad at me.

He stared at me for a moment, and for the first time since I'd known him, I felt uncomfortable. Caiden must have noticed, because he gave me a half-smile and put his arm around my waist, slamming Jackson's truck door shut behind us. Jackson glared at him for doing it, he babied that truck, and then started walking on my other side.

Jackson was wearing a tight navy V-neck shirt that showed off all the muscle he'd put on in spring training for football. He'd made Varsity as a freshman, the first guy to do that in five years, but then he'd sat the bench behind one of the seniors for most of the season, only getting some playing time the last two games when Christian, the senior receiver, had twisted his ankle. Jackson had kicked ass, and he'd had a fire lit under him to never sit the bench again. The results of that determination had been something to behold. He'd helped lead the team to a State Championship, and I knew Rutherford was chomping at the bit for him and Caiden to get there and start for their team.

I couldn't look away from the tan skin that was peeking out above his collar. The unbuttoned grey denim button-down he'd thrown on over his V-neck was pushed to his elbows, exposing thick forearms as if he was more professional athlete than sixteen-year-old boy. My heart started doing somersaults in my chest.

"Are you listening to me?" Caiden asked, a frustrated tinge to his tone. My cheeks flushed, and I quickly dragged my eyes away from Jackson to where Caiden's equally beautiful face waited impatiently for me to pay him attention.

"Hi," I whispered with a tentative smile, and his whole face softened as he flicked his gaze over my face, almost devouring my features. Something had changed between Caiden and I as well lately, and I wasn't sure how I felt about that.

The front of the school teemed with students who were all enjoying the warm weather. Everyone knew the last week of school was nothing but a way for the school to hit its state-mandated requirement for how many days we were supposed to attend, and it showed by the fact that half the school was still outside, even though the bell was going to ring at any minute.

The twins ignored everyone who was trying to get their attention, and we walked inside. Jackson took off his sunglasses once we got through the doors. It took me a minute before I saw his face, due to the distraction his perfectly muscled forearms gave me. When I did look at his face, a hot rush of disappointment mixed with fear crashed over me. Jackson's blue eyes were starting to darken. He was getting speedy.

I looked away from him quickly, not wanting to make him self-conscious. I was surprised that I hadn't noticed it in the car. Now that I was beside him, it was impossible not to notice all the signs I'd memorized over the years. His hand was beating a loud rhythm against his pants, and his attention was darting from one thing to another as we walked, not able to focus on anything for any length of time. There was even an extra skip in his step, and I had to walk faster to keep up with him.

When Jackson walked over to his locker, I pulled Caiden aside.

"He's speedy," I told him in a worried voice. Caiden looked over at Jackson as he hit his locker loudly after it wouldn't open.

"I know. But school should be chill this week. I'll watch him," he assured me. I nodded my head, a steady drum of unease nevertheless building up inside of me. I didn't want anything to ruin Jackson's summer or his chances at Rutherford. I knew his parents hadn't put bipolar down on Rutherford's medical form.

The twins both walked me to class before leaving for their own classes. Jackson had grabbed my hand as we were walking, and he gave it a squeeze and then me a wink as he walked away.

Donovan Tyler was on a tear today. Unfortunately, by some bad luck, he sat by me in most of my classes. Donovan happened to love to talk trash to everyone around him, and his favorite target was me. I hadn't told the guys about how bad it was getting. They were just words. I could handle them. I'd been through far worse.

Or at least, that was what my pep talk consisted of everyday as I listened to him.

"Heard your mama was sucking cock to keep a roof over your head, James," he whispered to me while the teacher was taking roll.

I studiously ignored him and began to read the next chapter of my history book.

"I bet she brings you in when her jaw gets tired," he continued.

I gazed even more intently at my history book, even as his words burned inside of me.

This continued throughout class, until I was at the point that if he said one more thing, I was going to throw my history book at his stupid, ugly face.

The bell saved us before my baser urges took over.

I hurried out of class, almost running into Jackson as he stood outside of my class, waiting for me while talking to some of his football buddies. They had been trying to get him to change his mind about Rutherford for months, even trying to get me to talk to him. Unfortunately for them, there wasn't any way on Earth that I would ever try and hold him back.

Jackson was bouncing on the balls of his feet, his features much more animated due to how speedy he was getting. Other people got excited when "social" Jackson came out to play, I only got ulcers.

"Wow, what's the rush, little angel?" he asked as he threw an arm around my waist, pulling me close. I took a moment to savor his smell, a mix of sandalwood and frankincense from the cologne he'd been using since he was twelve.

Opening my eyes, I tried to play it cool, knowing that if anyone was paying close attention they would think I was a freak...well, more of a freak than usual at least.

"Everything's fine," I squeaked, even as Donovan walked past us, throwing me a smirk.

Jackson happened to catch the look, and he glared hard at him, his left fist clenched as if he was holding himself back. "Is he bothering you, Eves?" he asked.

"It's nothing," I tried to say casually, but Jackson threw me a glance that let me know he could see right through me.

Caiden walked up to us just then, his lips pursing as he looked to where Jackson's arm was around me.

"Your girlfriend was looking pissy in class today, Jackson," Caiden said with a cruel grin. I stiffened.

Jackson rolled his eyes, indicating he knew exactly who Caiden was talking about. I was sure it was Veronica. "I'm surprised she wasn't all over you in class then, bro. You know how she likes brunettes," Jackson threw back, a warning in his voice.

There it was again, that strange tension that I'd noticed between the twins the last few weeks. What was going on with them?

Jackson's hand began to stroke the strip of skin that was peeking out between my shirt and my pants from my shirt riding up when I put my backpack on. Shivers cascaded down my spine, and Caiden definitely seemed to notice my reaction. His eyes darkened.

"See you guys later," he muttered before stalking off, making sure to smile sweetly at a group of junior cheerleaders as he did so.

I shook my head and watched him leave with a frown.

Jackson walked me to my next class by picking me up

and throwing me over his shoulder, ignoring my weak outrage when he did so. He sat me down in front of the door to my classroom and kissed my forehead. I was confident that butterflies were about to erupt out of my stomach. "See you at lunch, Eves," he smirked, before he walked away.

Psychology again had me sitting near Donovan, and he started the insults as soon as I walked in, asking me about all the dirty things I did with the twins. My nerves were shot by the time class ended and I was even tempted to say I was sick and go home, despite the hell that waited for me there.

I couldn't eat at lunch, and both Caiden and Jackson kept asking me what was wrong. Jackson kept throwing Donovan dirty looks where he was sitting at the table next to ours, suspicious that he was the culprit.

Donovan was an idiot. He had to be, because when I walked to the trashcan to throw away my still full lunch tray, he mouthed off to me again. "Your pussy must be real tight to keep both the twins coming to you. That's the only thing I can think of. Your pussy must be gold-plated."

Jackson happened to be stepping up to throw his tray away right as those words came out of Donovan's mouth.

That was his first mistake.

"You think you can talk to her like that?" Jackson screamed at Donovan. Jackson's normally blue eyes were so dark, they almost looked black. This was going to get out of control if Caiden or I didn't step in.

"Caiden, calm him down," I begged him. Caiden looked a little bit shell-shocked, and he made no immediate move to step in. Donovan got in Jackson's face, the wrong move for more reasons than one. "She's not sucking my dick," he taunted. "I don't have to forget that she's nothing but trash."

That was his last one. Jackson was on him, throwing him

to the ground as he started to throw punches at Donovan's face.

The first punch broke Donovan's nose, and blood started gushing out, splattering the front of his shirt.

"Stop," I screamed as I watched in terror, but Jackson was too far gone. He was lost to a place I couldn't find him. Punch after punch landed, until Donovan's face looked more like hamburger than human. *Finally*, Caiden stepped in and pulled Jackson off him.

Jackson was shaking, his eyes so dark, they resembled Caiden's. He tried to buck against Caiden's grip, and then teachers were running out, no doubt summoned by frantic students who'd run for help as soon as the fight began.

Horror gripped me as Mrs. Gomez, my English teacher, knelt by Donovan's side. "Someone call the authorities," she yelled frantically. There were multiple people on Jackson now, who was still out of control.

The next thirty minutes were awful. An ambulance arrived on site, and medical personnel rushed out wheeling a bed that they hurriedly placed Donovan on. Students were crying, and the teachers all looked scared.

Jackson had finally calmed down, but the damage had been done. The police arrived, and Jackson was handcuffed and led to a car. He looked back at me, a confused look on his face, as if he didn't know what had happened. Caiden came by my side and put his arm around my waist comfortingly as his twin shot him a look of betrayal.

I cried harder as they stuffed him into the car, and I buried my face in Caiden's neck as he stroked my hair and told me everything would be fine. I guess it should've registered that Caiden should have been calling his parents to help out his brother, but I was still shocked at what Jackson had just done.

I'd obviously seen his episodes before, but it wasn't until that moment that I saw how bad they could get.

After a life of constantly feeling out of control, I was rethinking everything. Out of control was literally written in Jackson's DNA. Jackson refused to take medicine, and I'd always supported him because I knew how numb it made him feel, but after seeing that...I didn't know what the answer was.

"You need to call your parents," I finally said, when I realized that Caiden still hadn't reached for his phone.

"The school already called them," he told me reassuringly. "Come on, let's get you home," he told me as he tried to lead me to the truck.

"No," I answered stubbornly. "We either have to go to the hospital to check on Donovan, or go to the police station and check on Jackson."

Something flashed in Caiden's eyes that I didn't recognize. "You're not going anywhere near that kid," he barked. "Not after what he said to you."

"Everyone says that about me," I glumly reminded him. "But it's my fault that he was injured like that. I should've done something to calm Jackson down."

"Fuck you should have," he answered tersely. "My brother's been getting more and more out of control. My parents have had to push more and more things under the rug. This wasn't your fault. Jackson needs to get his head out of his ass and take his medicine," Caiden growled, a fierce look on his face.

"He hates that stuff," I reminded him.

"You could've gotten hurt today. I don't care what that jackass wants," he responded. It was the first time I'd ever heard Caiden talk badly of Jackson, and it was unsettling. They'd always been a united front. Caiden the light to Jackson's complicated dark. It was weird to me to hear Caiden so angry with his brother.

"Let's go check on Jackson. We need to make sure that your parents actually get there. Didn't you say that they were about to leave on a trip?" I reminded him.

Caiden blew out an exasperated breath. "Dad did have a work trip. He's going to be furious, and not just because he's going to have to pay off Donovan's parents."

He led me to Jackson's truck, keeping his arm around me. Caiden opened my door for me and helped me in, since my legs still seemed to be made out of jelly. We were quiet on the way to the police station. Caiden put on my favorite song, and he reached across the center console to hold my hand. But instead of making me swoon like usual, the move felt wrong somehow, like it was premeditated. Almost like he was taking advantage of what happened with Jackson. I pushed the thought aside. That wasn't Caiden. Caiden loved his brother. He was just being there for me like always. Guilt assailed me for doubting him.

We got to the police station, and I was nervous about the twin's parents seeing me. They already disapproved of them spending so much time with me, and it was almost a guarantee that they would think that this was my fault. Which it was...

We walked in, and sure enough, the twin's parents were talking tersely with a man dressed in a sharp gray suit.

"That's Robert, our family attorney. It must be serious," Caiden whispered to me. He surprised me by taking my hand as we walked. His mother, Miranda, noticed it right away, and seemed to have trouble dragging her gaze from our clasped fingers.

"Your brother's really done it now," Mrs. Parker said with a grimace as she finally pulled her eyes to Caiden's face, patting his cheek gently. "Donovan's parents are already threatening a lawsuit, and the police are talking about charges of assault and battery," she said worriedly.

"Good," Caiden muttered, and both his mother and I jerked to look at him, shocked.

He shifted uncomfortably, as if he hadn't meant for that to escape his mouth.

"I didn't mean that," Caiden said quickly. "He just went too far today. He's getting worse."

Mrs. Parker wrung her hands. "He is. I don't know what to do," she said quietly, staring off into space. Abruptly, she must have remembered that I was standing there because she looked embarrassed to have said that in front of me.

"Everly, why don't you go on home, dear? I'm sure that Jackson will call you as soon as he's out," she told me in a nice voice that was obviously fake.

Caiden dropped my hand and put his arm around my waist again, pulling me towards him.

"She wants to stay, Mom," he said firmly, and his mother's mouth dropped. Mine did as well, because it very clearly felt like Caiden was claiming me in that moment.

And I didn't think that I wanted to be claimed.

I said nothing though, not wanting to make a scene. His mother must have been on my wavelength, because she sent Caiden a look that clearly said they would be talking about me later, and then she flashed me another fake smile.

"I'm going to go check in with the attorney," she said, turning and walking away.

Caiden led me over to a chair, and I sat down, chewing on my nails nervously as we waited.

"Surely your attorney can get Donovan's family to drop the charges. Especially after they find out that their son was bullying someone," I commented as I watched the officers at work around us.

Caiden didn't say anything, and I sat up straighter at how contemplative he seemed.

"It will be alright," I reassured him. "Jackson always gets himself out of these things," I told him, assuming he was worried about his twin.

"I think Jackson has gotten too out of control for you to be around him anymore by yourself," he blurted out.

I looked at him like he was crazy. "Caiden, you know that he would never hurt me," I exclaimed. "He was defending me today. It was wrong what he did. But he'll learn from this. He can come back from it."

Caiden was already shaking his head before I was finished speaking. "There are things you don't know about Jackson," he told me. "Remember that Tamara girl in your physics class last fall...?"

"Yes," I responded slowly, not understanding what he was getting at.

"He took her on a date in October and things went too far. He ended up hurting her when she said no," Caiden said somberly, as if he was embarrassed to have to tell me.

My mouth opened in shock. "Caiden, you don't actually believe that," I scolded him. "Jackson would never do that."

He just shook his head at my response, pursing his lips angrily. We didn't talk much after that. He stayed stuck to my side like glue, which normally I wouldn't mind, but all I wanted to do in that moment was talk to Jackson. Their mother finally came to my rescue.

"Caiden, let's go. We're going to grab something to eat with Robert. The Chief of Police just left for dinner, and we're going to have a little run in with him," she said. It was obvious what "run in" meant. One good thing about the rich,

Jackson would be getting out of jail sooner rather than later, and probably without anything on his record. For a second, I thought about Donovan's broken face that would likely never be the same again, but I quickly pushed the image out of my head.

I would always be on Jackson's and Caiden's side.

"Everly's coming with us," said Caiden, reaching for my hand, again. Luckily for me, his mother was already shaking her head.

"You need to do this for your brother. And Everly needs to go home. The police told us that this happened because Jackson was defending Everly," she said disapprovingly.

Caiden opened his mouth to object again, but I touched his shoulder softly. "I need to get home anyway. Call me later?"

"How are you going to get home?" Caiden asked.

"My mom will come get me," I lied. Caiden looked at me like he didn't believe me. And he shouldn't. But he decided to let it go. I doubt he would be able to convince his parents that I needed to be driven home first.

I pretended to walk out with them, and then as soon as they got into Mr. Parker's Mercedes and left, I looked around and went back into the police station. I wasn't sure why I was there. I highly doubted that they were going to let me see Jackson.

Employees in the police department gave me questioning glances as I sat there, but I ignored them.

Hours passed, and finally an employee came over to me. "Darlin', do we need to call your parents?" she asked.

"I'm just waiting for news about Jackson Parker," I murmured sleepily.

"Jackson Parker was let go an hour ago," she responded with a frown.

I sat up straighter in my chair "How did I miss him?"

"There's a separate entrance out back. The chief himself took him through there. I'm sure he's home by now."

I nodded, standing up. I was sore from sitting on that hard chair, but relieved that Jackson had been released. It definitely paid to be rich.

It was a long walk home.

<hr />

I WAS at the twin's house bright and early the next morning. Caiden had texted me at midnight saying that Jackson had gotten home. I wasn't sure why he told me hours after Jackson had been released. But I guess they would all have been busy dealing with the fallout.

Jackson was suspended for the last few days of school, but all the charges against him had been dropped. It helped that he was a minor as well. The police were able to classify the fight as just "rough play" around the schoolyard, although that was the most ridiculous way to describe what had happened that I'd ever heard.

I timed my arrival at the twin's house for when I knew Caiden would be at soccer practice. As I knocked on the door, I just hoped that it would be their butler who answered and not one of their parents.

To my surprise, a tired looking Jackson opened the door. For a moment, he looked relieved to see me, but then the look disappeared off his face, and there was just blankness.

"Everly, you need to go home," he told me as he tried to close the door in my face.

I put my hand out to stop the door, and Jackson stopped pushing on it, not wanting to hurt me.

"Let me come in," I begged. I hated the vibe I was getting between us.

"Everly, I'm tired. We can talk later."

I knew that if we didn't talk right now, whatever was going on between us would just get worse.

"You're not allowed to shut me out Jackson Parker," I scolded him, pushing my way inside. Jackson rolled his eyes as he opened the door, but there was a hint of a smile on his face.

I expected him to take me to his room where we usually hung out when we were alone, but instead, he took me to the living room. The dread I had been feeling since the fight only intensified as he sat in a chair a few feet away from the couch I was sitting on like he was desperate for space.

"What's going on?" I asked nervously, fiddling with the hem of my shirt.

"Everly, I didn't want to have to even talk about this. But I guess you're going to make it awkward for both of us?"

Apprehension curled up in my stomach.

"I just wanted to make sure you were alright after what happened."

He pushed a frustrated hand through his hair that looked more blonde than gold right now under the sun that was shining through the window. His eyes were still darker than normal, showing he was still coming out of an episode.

"Eves, you've got to let this little crush you have on me, go," he said carefully, his hands beating out a nervous rhythm on his legs as he spoke. He looked me straight in the eye, and there was no sign on his face that he was kidding.

My mouth dropped open. A little crush? Was he not present at his birthday party? Was he not a willing accomplice to that kiss? A kiss I'd been obsessing about since it happened.

"Don't look at me like that," he responded with a sigh. "I was drunk at that party. And you'd been staring at me like a kicked puppy all night. I shouldn't have given in."

My whole body shook with rage. I wanted to punch him in the fucking face.

"You self-indulgent prick. You were not drunk. Don't try and pussy your way out of this because you're scared, Jackson," I raged at him.

He kept the same, stoic, stupid face as I yelled.

"Everly, just drop it. I'm your friend, so I should be able to tell you when you're being pathetic."

His words sliced into me, carving up my heart into little pieces and scattering them in the wind. "Maybe we should just have some space for a while until you get over the unfortunate feelings you think you have."

"Unfortunate feelings..." I whispered as I looked at him disbelievingly. Who was this person sitting in front of me? Since the day I'd met him, there hadn't been a day where Jackson hadn't wanted to see me. "If that's what you think," I finally said stiffly. "You know better than anyone that I don't like to be where I'm not wanted."

He flinched from that barbed statement, but I didn't care. I headed towards the door, numb...feeling like my whole life had been rearranged in a moment. I stopped in front of the door. "You're a coward, Jackson Parker, or you wouldn't have done this. Don't bother trying to come for me when you get over whatever this was," I warned him angrily. And I meant it. Even with all the shit I'd experienced over the years, no one had hurt me as bad as what he'd just done.

I was already missing him as I slammed the door behind me. I heard something crash from inside, but I didn't go back in to check on what had happened. He deserved every feeling that he was experiencing right now.

Heartbreak Prince

I was so lost in my misery that I smacked right into a hard chest.

"Woah, there, LyLy. What's going on? What are you doing here?" Caiden asked. I looked at him with watery eyes. "Wow...baby. What's wrong?" His face curled up in distress and then anger. "What did that fucking asshole do now?" he hissed, letting me go as he prepared to march inside to confront Jackson.

I held up my hands to stop him beseechingly. "It's fine. It was obviously something I needed to hear."

"He shouldn't have said something to hurt your feelings. He's an idiot."

A hiccupping sob rushed out of my mouth.

He pulled me back towards his chest and softly rubbed my back. I felt so worthless. So lonely. For so long, Jackson had always been there. I'd never imagined a day when he didn't want to be. Maybe there really was something wrong with me.

"Shhh, baby. Whatever you're thinking, stop it." I looked up at him with watery eyes. "Want to get out of here?" he asked, his eyes flicking all over my face.

I nodded numbly, and he slid his arm around me as he led me to his Jeep.

We were quiet as we drove, and I wasn't even paying attention to where we were going. My mind was racing over every detail of my interactions with Jackson since the kiss. *Why was he doing this? It wasn't like it was the first time he'd gotten in a fight because of something someone said about me. Maybe that was it. Maybe he was tired of getting in trouble for me. But it wasn't like I had ever once asked him to fight or even stand up for me. And when he was speedy, he got into fights about everything.*

"Everly!" Caiden's voice bit through the turmoil coursing

through my mind. I looked over at him in the driver's seat where he was staring at me concerned. I offered him a weak smile.

"Let's go for a walk," he suggested as he shut off the car. I looked around and realized that we were by the lake at one of my favorite spots to come with the guys.

We got out of the car, and Caiden grabbed my hand as he led me over to the walking trail that led around the entire lake. Our walk was silent for a while, but being outside surrounded by nature was doing the trick. I could feel myself relaxing.

"I knew you would like this," commented Caiden, and I looked over at him and saw him watching me. I felt shy under his gaze.

"It's always nice to be out here."

He stopped us and turned to face me, looking nervous.

Caiden slowly pulled a piece of hair away from my face carefully, as if I was liable to run with any sudden movement. "Everly," he whispered, leaving me shaky under the intensity of his voice.

"You know I'll always be with you. You'll never be alone." His hand trailed from the side of my face, down my neck, and then down my arm, leaving a trail of tingles in its wake. "I'm in love with you," he continued.

I didn't understand at that moment how I could feel so much dread and anticipation at the same time. This was Caiden though. He'd been my best friend just as long as Jackson. He was sweet and sunny...and stable. He would never let me down. And I did love him. I loved almost everything about him.

It just wasn't the same as what I thought I'd been feeling about Jackson.

But maybe that wasn't the kind of love I should be going

after. After all, it was my dad's passionate personality that led him to kill himself.

Desperate love was dangerous.

What I needed was a steady kind of love. A love that would never let me down.

So when Caiden leaned down to kiss me, I let him. And it was a good kiss. A great one probably. Just not the kind that set my soul on fire.

I told myself that it was okay for it to feel like that.

And I ignored the fact that Jackson's face kept creeping into my mind throughout the kiss.

⁂

IT WASN'T Jackson that was selfish. It was me. Me and my fear of being alone.

I ruined three lives that day.

If only I'd known.

10

NOW

I saw Jackson everywhere. And he, in turn, pretended that he never saw me. He ignored me for the whole next week. It was like he hadn't woken up in my bed at all.

No matter what he did though, I wanted him.

Damn heart, I needed a new one, because his one had to be defective. It kept breaking into pieces each time I saw him or heard his voice. I was still reeling from the imprudent feelings my traitorous body insisted upon when he'd wrapped me in his arms that night. I couldn't seem to forget his touch and the butterflies merrily danced in my stomach each time he was near me — even when he was flirting with every girl in the vicinity.

"What's with the long face?" Landry asked me as he set his tray down on my table and slid into the seat next to me.

I couldn't help but smile at the grin he gave me. His eye looked slightly better after a week. It was now more a greenish color instead of the black and blue it had been at first.

"Oh, you know, not getting a lot of sleep trying to keep up with classes. They've already piled on the homework."

"They kill us here, don't they?" he agreed with a smile as he took a bite of his hamburger. "You know, we could study together sometime. I'm sure I've taken quite a few of your classes, and I could help you out."

I grinned at his offer. I'd never gotten below an A in my life, but I also hadn't had a friend to study with since Caiden and Jackson...

Speaking of Jackson, he was standing just a few feet away. He'd been flirting with a black-haired girl for the last fifteen minutes —I was beginning to think intentionally — but now his focus was one hundred percent on Landry and me. And he did not look happy.

That made me angry. Because really. How the fuck, dare he? What right did he have to look upset about me talking to someone? The Jackson that I'd use to know would have wanted me to have as many friends as I could.

Well, maybe as many girlfriends as I could...

But that was beside the point.

"Can you study tonight?" I asked Landry, shooting him a grin. I only felt a little bad about the somewhat ulterior motives I had at the moment.

"Awesome," he said, and a little piece of me melted. Landry really did seem like a great guy.

If only I wasn't hopelessly infected by the asshole staring daggers at me right now.

A group of Landry's hockey teammates arrived at the table, and that was my cue to leave. I wasn't ever going to feel comfortable around large groups of people after what I'd been subjected to my whole life. Parties were a bit easier because people were busy doing their own thing, but there was too much of a chance I'd have them all paying attention to me if I stayed at the table.

"Leaving?" Landry complained as he stuck his lip out in a ridiculous pout.

It was something that Caiden would have done, and my heart clenched.

Landry watched my face, confused. I knew pain was written across it.

"Text me when you're ready to study tonight," I told him hurriedly, wanting to get away fast so I wasn't splayed open in front of him. He'd gotten my number a few days earlier when he'd accosted me in the hallway, but so far, he hadn't used it in a way that made me uncomfortable.

I had to walk past Jackson to get out of the cafeteria, and I happened to trip over someone's backpack that someone had splayed out in the aisle right as I passed him.

I fell to a knee on my bad leg, grimacing as it hit the hard marble floor. And yes, I did attend a school that had a marble floor in its fucking cafeteria.

Suddenly, a hand reached out to help me up. It was Jackson's of course.

"Everly," he said roughly, as he looked at me through his lashes that every girl would die to have. I'd thought often growing up though that death by Jackson Parker would be a gift. He bit his bottom lip, and I thought about how I would like to replace his teeth with mine.

Damn, this had to stop. The intensity, the feels, the tingly sensation lighting up my spine, all of it, so I quickly pulled my hand away from his after he helped me up and tried to limp out of the cafeteria with a modicum of dignity.

He stayed with me, his hand on the small of my back to guide me past the entry and through a less populated passage of the school hallway.

"Haven't gotten any more graceful over the last few years," he commented dryly, but I could almost sense his smile, even though I kept my gaze firmly focused in front of me. And I was pretty sure that smile was ending with a dimple that broke hearts everywhere.

"Ignoring me?" he asked, sounding amused. And that did it. I whirled around to face him, gritting my teeth because my leg hurt like a bitch. I was furious. Furious because he was impossible to ignore. Furious because I'd never before felt anything close to the longing he'd built deep within my heart, and furious because he was such an asshole.

I took a deep breath before I spoke because I knew that he'd been trying to get a rise out of me. "I'm pretty sure out of the two of us, you're the one who's been ignoring me," I responded calmly, even as I devoured the planes of his face.

He stared at me just as intensely.

Jackson stepped closer to me, taunting me with the heat radiating from his chest. "You've missed me. Haven't you, little devil?" he said, holding me firmly with his gaze while our bodies remained a millimeter apart.

"What do you want, Jackson?" I responded desperately.

"For some reason, I can't stay away from you. I've tried, Everly. I have, but each time I see you, I'm drawn back in, even though I know I should stay away. You're like the sweetest poison." His head dipped, and my knees weakened. Without thought, I reached for his hair. The silken length slipped through my fingers, and I fisted it. Oh, fuck. I pulled, drawing him closer still, and the connection felt... right, like my hands were meant to live in the soft waves.

A low rumble vibrated into me, and he lowered his lips to hover directly over mine. He inhaled deeply, slowly and methodically, taking my breath into him as if I was the last whisper of oxygen to fill his lungs. Moving a fraction, his lips brushed against my cheek, and my heart galloped. I couldn't think—the only thing running through my head was please, please kiss me.

"Everly." He murmured my name as his nose ran along the line of my jaw, rubbing delicately against my skin. His hands, which had remained by his side, moved to my nape. His fingers dug into my hair to hold me steady, but even without them, I wouldn't move, I couldn't move. Everything was so soft, light, a teasing need. He was on a slow, deliberate path, tracing his lips and nose along every inch of my face, breathing in every minute detail as his thumbs drew a delicate line along my lips.

"Jackson, please." To my horror I'd whispered it out loud, and although it was barely spoken, the words seemed to echo throughout the hallway. For the briefest moment, he pressed his lips against my forehead, holding me tight against him.

"I'm sorry," he said, pulling away. My hands fell indelicately to my sides, empty and wanting. "I won't ever forgive you for what you've done. This... us... can't happen." His lids fell closed for the briefest second, as if the words hurt him as much as they did me.

And then he was gone, and I was left trembling in the hallway.

Jackson Parker would never stop ruining me.

§

It felt like people were staring at me in the library. And it didn't seem like it was because I was with Landry...who was, by the way, still a sweetheart. He'd brought snacks. How could I not like him?

"We may need to book a new study room in the future,"

commented Landry as he looked around. And I was glad he'd just confirmed I wasn't going crazy.

"There needs to be a little more studying and not so much staring," I agreed, glaring back at a group of girls who were sitting a few tables over, obviously gossiping about me.

"You know, we could study at the hockey house sometime, too," he commented casually, as if he was just throwing out the idea.

I gritted my teeth. "I doubt I would be able to study there."

He made a non-committal sound. "Well, what if we didn't study...and we just hung out?" he asked.

My shoulders clenched, because I had really been hoping that he would hold off on asking me out for a date and I could enjoy having another friend for a little while longer.

I opened my mouth to shut him down, but then I snapped it shut. Why should I say no? Because of another round of hot and cold with Jackson? The fact that we had history wasn't going to stop him from hating me. Maybe it would be good for me to get out there. To see what life was like outside of a Parker boy.

I was just about to say yes when my phone buzzed in my pocket. "Hold that thought," I told him with what I hoped looked like a sexy smile.

My smile quickly faded though when I saw who it was. Jackson.

He hadn't texted me in two years, and I almost dropped my phone.

I need to see you. Meet me on the side of Stanton Hall.

My heart raced. I shouldn't go. I knew that, especially

after what he'd done to me earlier. I had just gone through the reasons why I should be saying yes to a date with Landry and getting off the crazy train that was anything to do with Jackson. But my stupid, stupid heart wouldn't listen.

"I've got to go. I need to talk to a professor during her office hours," I told Landry, packing up my books. He seemed shocked, and a bit crestfallen.

I started to walk away, and then I whirled around. "Hanging out sounds good though, Landry," I said softly, and his face melted into a grin.

"Okay, sweetheart," he responded. And then I was off.

I walked across campus, shivering as I went. The nights were growing cool and I would need to start taking a jacket with me if I was going to be late. I looked at the text Jackson had sent again, wondering why he wanted to meet up with me. Had that confession earlier been an opening for us to actually talk about everything? My heart leapt hopefully at the thought.

When I got to the side of Stanton Hall, he wasn't there though. There were a few bags of trash on this side of the building, and a small set of doors encased by concrete on the ground that looked like they led to a cellar or something under the building. I grew uneasy.

It was a bad idea to come; I did have some sense of self-preservation. But some piece of me that belonged to Jackson no matter what he did had made me do it. I leaned against the wall of the building and tried to calm down, even as my heart threatened to leap out of my chest.

There was only one small floodlight on this side of the building, and even though it wasn't all the way dark yet, it still made me uneasy to be all alone. I had pulled out my phone to text Jackson and ask where he was when I heard something crash behind the dumpster, making me jump.

"Jackson," I called out uneasily, turning to see if I could see anything. I was going to run out of here in about two seconds if he didn't appear.

The sounds coming from behind the dumpster distracted me until it was too late. I'd just heard the footsteps coming from behind me when a bag was thrown over my head and at least one pair of hands scooped me up and started to walk with me while I screamed and cursed and tried to get away. My backpack and phone were ripped away from me.

This was not happening to me. I was not about to get kidnapped because of my hapless obsession with a boy.

But whoever had me didn't seem interested in kidnapping me. They had something else planned for me that honestly...might have been worse.

A heavy set of doors thudded against the ground as someone opened them up, and I shivered. Because I knew exactly where those doors were and what these creeps had planned for me. Whoever had me started to walk down a set of stairs, and I could feel the air getting cooler as we went underground. I began to thrash even harder. My nails managed to gouge into my captor's chest, breaking their skin, and I heard a muffled "Fuck" from a voice I didn't recognize.

I was thrown to the ground, shocks of pain once again shooting through my poor leg. The person started to climb back up the stairs and I tried to scramble behind them blindly. I tripped on something though and fell back to the ground, and that was enough time for the person to get up the stairs, and the doors to the room to slam closed above me.

I ripped off the bag on my head and gasped as I realized

that the room was just as dark as the bag had been. I was locked in a fucking cellar of some kind.

Tears raged down my cheek as I forced myself to crawl up the stairs to the doors so that I could try and open them. Had Jackson done this? He had to have been a part of it, even though obviously, he wasn't working alone.

He knew I hated the dark. He knew about the nightmares I'd had as a child. How my mother used to throw me in a dark closet for punishment, and how I'd scream and scream to be let out.

I beat on the door, screaming until my voice was hoarse for someone to let me out. At first, there was laughter from the other side, but it had faded as they had left. I tried to beat on the door more, but eventually, the fear of not being able to see what was behind me pushed me to try and find a wall to sit against so that at least nothing could approach me from behind.

I rocked back and forth against that wall, the dark slowly trying to drive me mad. It was so dark in this room that we must have been underground. The dirt floor I sat on reinforced that, and I shivered to think of what creepy crawlies were scuttling around me. It was so dark that I couldn't even see how big the room was.

That obsession that I'd felt for so long about Jackson...it started to fade in that dark room, until it resembled something that felt a lot like hate.

※

IT WAS A LONG NIGHT. Maybe the longest one of my life.

I was scared of the dark because of what my mother did to me growing up, but I was also scared of the dark because that was where every bad thought I'd ever had took cover.

Most of my bad thoughts consisted of my father and the twins. Caiden was behind every shadow, my father was in every one of my nightmares, and Jackson...he was the devil in the corner that used to be an angel.

Like I said, I hated the dark.

The cold of the ground eventually seeped into my skin until I was a shivering, shaking mess.

I'd been bullied all my life. I'd developed quite the tough skin. But whatever was happening here was a kind of psychological torture I wasn't prepared for.

The night was endless. Every creak and groan I heard made me jump. I prayed to God for the first time in years, when a small sliver of daylight finally peeked in between the crack of the two doors. But at this point, my throat was too hoarse and sore to muster anything but a faint "Help me." It was definitely not loud enough to actually do any good.

I was in that cellar for so long that I started to wonder if this went beyond bullying. What if I was just left down here permanently, and they found my body years down the road when someone happened to come down here for a miscellaneous tool?

Would Jackson kill me if given the chance? Just like how I basically killed his brother?

I'd started to spiral even more when suddenly, there was a clanging sound from up above me, and one of the cellar doors suddenly opened with a loud crash.

A shocked looking man dressed in a school janitor's jumpsuit appeared, and he almost jumped out of his skin when he saw me sobbing at the foot of the stairs.

"What are you doing down there, girl?" he cried out, rushing down the stairs to help me up. My limbs were numb from sitting on the cold ground, and my leg was worse than it had been in a long time.

"I was locked down here," I explained in between stuttering sobs. He led me up the stairs and then pulled out his walkie-talkie to ask someone to get someone from the administration to meet us at the nurse's office.

"There's my backpack," I sniffled, pointing a few feet away where it had been thrown. I was never going to put my phone in my backpack again.

He offered to carry me when he saw how badly I was limping, but students were already starting to mill about for breakfast before the first classes of the day started, and I didn't want to garner even more attention than I already was in my bedraggled, limping state.

My whole goal upon coming to school was to stay under the radar, get my classes done, get into the university, and start the future that I hoped was waiting for me somewhere out there.

My goals were quickly being blown to bits.

I'd tried to stop crying as we walked, but my stupid leg hurt so much that I was a crying mess by the time we made it. A concerned nurse quickly led me to a bed, and I laid there, cursing the world until someone from the administration came into the room.

From the look of her, she'd seen my file, knew exactly what kind of family I'd come from, and immediately decided that I was the trouble, somehow bringing things like this upon myself.

Fortunately for me, the nurse stayed hovering nearby, and so she had to pretend to somewhat give a shit. "So you're saying that you were walking around last night and you got thrown into the gardening cellar by an unknown assailant... Where were you walking to?"

Yes, I knew I was the dumbest girl on the planet before I even opened my mouth, because for some reason, I couldn't tell her that it was Jackson. I didn't know if it was pride in not wanting to tell on someone, or if it was a habit from years filled with always having Jackson's back. But I just couldn't bring myself to tell her that I was supposed to be meeting him.

"I was on my way back to my dorm from the library," I told her, and the lie tasted sour on my lips.

She made a non-committal humming sound, like she didn't believe me, or she thought that I had far more nefarious reasons for walking around last night. But she didn't say anything more on the subject.

"Well, we will definitely look into this. Why don't you get some pain medicine now and take the day off from classes?" she suggested as she stood up and brushed non-existent wrinkles off her plaid power suit.

"Thank you," I responded listlessly as the nurse brought over some Advil. It would barely take the edge off the pain, but my pain relievers were in my room, so it would have to do for now.

I lay on that bed in the nurse's station for half the day.

I would've gone home if I'd had a home to go to.

Melanie was painting her nails with a friend when I finally made it back to my room. I needed to shower badly, but I wasn't so sure that a snake or something else wouldn't be released in my stall again just to torture me further, and I didn't have it in me to be brave.

"Where have you been?" she asked, wrinkling her nose.

I fell on my bed, not bothering to answer her. I listened to them whispering about me for about half a second before I fell into a blissfully dreamless sleep.

I HADN'T MEANT to come to his room again. But like I said, habits are hard to break.

He lay there unchanged, and I sat there just staring at him, wondering what my life would be like right now if that summer had never happened.

He was still beautiful, even in his sleep. His muscles had shrunk from years of inactivity, but his face was still a work of art.

"You got what you wanted, you know. He hates me," I whispered to him as the machines around him beeped slowly.

But of course, he didn't answer.

A part of me almost envied him. He didn't have to face any repercussions from what happened that night. He went from one of the state's football heroes to some kind of tragic hero while I was left in the ashes. What would it be like to avoid all responsibility for every flawed thing you'd ever done?

I didn't think I'd ever find out.

I got up from the chair I'd been perched on beside his bed and didn't bother to say goodbye, or that I wouldn't be back.

Because now it would be a lie.

I was never going to be able to move past Caiden and what I'd done.

11

I was going on a date with Landry that evening. We were in Lane's room to avoid Melanie, and Lane flitted around me like I was the Barbie doll she'd always wanted to play with. It was five days after the cellar incident. I'd done nothing but go to class and return to my room.

Lane had finally staged an intervention, bringing Chinese takeout and *Steel Magnolias* to my room the night before. I'd been avoiding her, but once she was there, the whole sordid story had come out. Well...at least some parts of the story. I'd never tell anyone what happened that night with Caiden. It was enough for her to know that I'd once dated him, and that Jackson held me responsible for his injuries. Lane had tried to press for more, but I'd already given her more than I'd uttered to another living person. She'd obviously been concerned about the fact that I'd been thrown into a cellar and wanted to call the police, but I'd convinced her not to. I didn't tell her that I'd had to buy a flashlight and keep it on next to me when I tried to sleep, because I was even more terrified of the dark than ever before.

She'd retaliated by forcing me to return Landry's call, and now here I was, getting ready to go on a date with him. My first date in two years in fact.

She had an entire basket worth of beauty products spread out on her bed, and I stared at all the items she was laying out, a bit terrified. I'd never had this kind of experience. You know, the one where you actually have a friend to talk about makeup and beauty tips with. Lane was trying to explain to me the art of contouring at the moment, and it was going straight over my head.

"Maybe we should just stick with some eyeliner and some mascara and call it good," I told her as she came at me with something she called a "blurring stick."

"This comes with the territory of being friends with me, babe," she snorted as she dropped the blurring stick and picked up a brush and some powder instead. I could do powder.

"I'm nervous," I blurted out. "I can't believe I'm doing this. What if it sucks?"

She set the powder brush down and went over to her cabinet where she pulled out a bottle of vodka and two shot glasses. "You need a little of this to relax," she stated calmly as she poured the shots and handed one to me. Today, her hair was up in a messy bun that looked like it would be impossible to replicate. She had two chopsticks in it that were somehow holding it up, and she was wearing a black shirt with Thor on it that said, "You want me to put the hammer down?" over bright blue leggings and combat boots.

She was effortlessly cool, and I still didn't know what in the world she was doing hanging out with me.

"We're going to play a game—two truths, and a lie. We'll

both offer up our truths and lies and if you guess wrong, you have to drink a shot."

"Pretty sure that you're not supposed to show up for a date drunk," I commented with a laugh, knowing that I was going to play the game.

"We still have two hours. We'll play for thirty minutes, and then you can sober up. Just try not to guess wrong too much," she giggled.

I rolled my eyes. "Okay, you go first."

"*Okay*," she said, pursing her lips as she thought about what to say. "Alright. My favorite color is black. I had a dog growing up named Barnie. And my favorite movie is *Legally Blonde*."

I scoffed. "Obviously, your favorite movie is not *Legally Blonde*."

A triumphant grin lit up her face. "Got you. My favorite color is actually pink. Everything else was true."

My mouth dropped open. "Your favorite color is pink? You're like, destroying your image right now."

She giggled. "Drink up, bitch."

I threw the shot back and gasped as it burned my throat. I was so not a drinker.

"Your turn," she sang at me. I cleared my throat as I thought about what I was going to say.

"I hate grape jelly. I sing in the shower. And I want to go to medical school," I told her.

She fiddled with some more makeup as she thought about my three things. "Ahah. It's that you want to go to medical school. That's the lie. You're in all English classes."

I grinned. "Nope, my lie was that I hate grape jelly," I said with a laugh as she grumbled and took her shot.

"But you love books," she pouted. "Why are you taking all

college English courses if you're just going to take all science classes once you get into the college?"

I hadn't meant for this to become a deep discussion. "I want to be rich, and English majors don't get rich," I said lamely, even though that was a lie. I wasn't going to tell her that I wanted to be a doctor so that maybe I could help Caiden or others like him someday. I would never tell anyone that.

"Oh," she said, clearly disappointed in my answer.

"What are you majoring in?" I asked, cocking my head.

Her eyes lit up. "Oh, I'm a music major and an English minor. I sing and play five different instruments. The minor is to help with my songwriting. Someday, I'm going to make it big," she explained as her eyes went a bit dreamy.

There was silence for a minute, as if she was imagining her future, and then she snapped back to life. "Alright, we need to keep going," she said, bouncing on her toes.

And so we did. And I found out that I liked Lane even more after learning so many inane details about her, like the fact that she hated oranges, drank at least five cups of coffee a day, and had been to six of the seven continents.

She really was a crazy cool girl.

And I found out she was really good at makeup, even while tipsy. As I looked in the mirror, you couldn't even tell that I hadn't slept well in weeks. My eyes were artfully done in golds and browns, making my blue eyes pop. She'd managed to contour my face like a pro, and I felt a bit like Kim Kardashian staring at her work.

My phone rang. Crap, it was already time for Landry to pick me up. "I'll be right out," I rushed into the phone, before hanging up and throwing it onto the bed like a psycho. It was a struggle to put on the black mini dress that Lane had forced me to borrow. After the accident, I'd worn nothing but long pants due to the thick scar that extended from my ankle to my knee, but I'd eventually gotten over that. It wasn't like I could hide the fact that I had a limp, so why should I hide the scar that showed the injury that made me limp?

I was definitely a bit tipsy as I left Lane's room to meet Landry in the common room where he'd texted he was waiting. It was exactly the liquid courage that I needed though.

He looked good. He was wearing a sage green button-up that made his eyes pop even more, with a pair of dark, fitted jeans. His russet-colored hair was done in that artfully messy way that all guys seemed to be able to master.

His eyes lit up when he saw me. "You look great," he stammered, and his cheeks got a little red as he looked me up and down. It was definitely something to see this striking, popular guy a little twitterpated because of someone like me.

"You don't look too shabby yourself," I said as I gave him a corny grin, and his whole face brightened with his megawatt smile.

He led me to his car, a shiny red muscle car that I couldn't name, but I knew was expensive.

I took a deep breath as I slid into the leather seat. I always got a little nervous in cars ever since the accident. It was better when I could drive and have control. I practiced my breaths so that I could stay calm and not let my freak flag fly so soon into the date.

"I made reservations at my favorite Italian place. Is that alright?" he asked, suddenly looking worried, like I was going to tell him that I hated Italian.

"I love Italian. I've never met a carb that I didn't trust," I told him seriously, and he laughed, sounding a bit awestruck at my comment.

We made small talk about classes and hockey as we drove. The restaurant was nearby, so it didn't take long to get there.

It looked like a nice place, one of those authentic Italian places that made their pasta from scratch. There was a line of people waiting outside to get in, and I was grateful for the reservation since we would have had to wait for hours otherwise.

A hostess who had all the eyes for Landry immediately seated us, and I teased him about it mercilessly after we were sat at our table.

The waiter suggested calamari for the appetizer, and we immediately dug in as soon it was brought to the table, finding lots to talk and joke about as we both ate.

It was shaping up to be a really good date.

But of course, really good things were never allowed to happen to me.

Jackson walked in with two of his football friends that I'd seen him with, and they all had dates. Jackson was with a tall, thin, red-headed beauty I immediately hated on sight.

The hostess showed his group to a table a few tables away from us, and I shrunk against my bench seat, praying that he wouldn't see me.

"You've got to be shitting me," muttered Landry as he angrily eyed Jackson's group. "Do we need to leave?" he asked, and I looked at him confused.

His face softened. "Everly, I'm not sure what kind of bullshit Parker was trying to play at the other day, but it's obvious that he not only knows you, but that you have quite the history."

My lip quivered. "Quite the history" was an understatement.

"Whatever was between us is over now," I told him, even though the statement felt hollow as it passed from my lips.

"Okay, I just don't want to play a game where I don't know all the players," Landry said gruffly, and I smiled at his sports analogy.

"Let's just have a good time," I told him, and Landry smiled.

"Sounds good."

Our entrees were brought to the table. I'd ordered chicken parmesan, and Landry had ordered baked ziti and Caesar salad. We continued to make small talk, but whatever easiness we'd had before was gone. At least for me.

I could literally feel Jackson's hot gaze on me as I tried to eat. I swore he was talking louder than usual just so I could hear him. When I did happen to glance over to their table, Jackson made sure he was touching his date, who of course was melting from his attention.

I don't know what I thought would happen when I came to Rutherford. But I hadn't expected this. Was it always going to be like this?

I finally couldn't take it anymore. It was like the air in the room had become suffocating. Landry looked at me concerned. "I just need to use the ladies' room," I said shakily, and he nodded, although I could tell that he was annoyed, there was a tightness around his eyes that hadn't been there before Jackson had arrived. Jackson ruined everything.

Making sure not to look at his table, I all but ran to the bathroom.

The bathroom was blissfully empty, and I stood in front of the sink staring at my pale complexion in the bathroom mirror. I took a deep sigh, and then I turned on the water to splash some on my face.

The door opened behind me.

And then, there he was.

We just stared at each other through the mirror for a long moment. He was breathing heavily, like he'd just gotten done running.

I finally came to my senses and spun around. "Get out of here," I hissed. "It's bad enough you're even in the same restaurant as me."

"Did you really think I wasn't going to find out that you were going on a date?" He laughed cruelly.

I groaned. "Why does it matter, Jackson? You hate me. So why can't you just let me go?" The last part of my sentence comes out as a desperate, bleating, whisper.

Then, suddenly he was there, right in front of me. He pulled me toward him. The scent of him rushed over me, and I should've pushed him away.

But I couldn't

This was heaven. This was hell.

This was everything.

"What makes you think that I'll ever let you go?" His sensual tone and the seductive way he worked my body stole my gasp. He sucked and licked along my neck, my pulse careening out of control beneath his magical tongue. His touch burned through my veins, heating to a boiling point of lust. I was drunk with desire, whimpering as his fevered hot kisses on my searing flesh instantly spiked my need for him.

"Do you think you'll ever get over me?" he whispered huskily, brushing past my lips with his to continue his teasing along my jaw, his hand slipping under my dress to slide along my saturated core. "Were you this wet for him?" he growled with a harsh grope of my sex. I moaned at the touch, my pussy clenching in desperate need for him, pulsing uncontrollably at the claim of his hand before he abruptly pulled it away.

Its sudden absence jarred my lust-filled haze as he placed his hand on the wall, caging my gaze to his, locked onto his brilliant, angry, blue eyes. "You'll always be mine, Everly. Even when I don't want you," he growled.

He took my lips, his tongue invaded my mouth as he cupped my face, tilting my head to give him better access. I trembled in his grip, falling mercy to his attack. How easily I lost myself in him. I kissed him back with a vengeance, hungry and desperate to reclaim what was mine— the sudden need catapulting me into the heavens and back.

I wrenched myself away from him. Both of us were breathing heavy now. For several seconds, minutes even, as though the Earth stopped on its axis, we stared at each other amid panting anger and craving. We were trapped beneath a ferocious tidal wave of desire; frozen, looming above us, around us, and we both knew it was about to come crashing down to drown us in its lustful fury.

I sensed the moment Jackson was about to pounce, the moment my eyes secretly, silently, whispered so much more than any words ever could. I wanted him now. As much as he wanted me. He reached for me, his attack viciously laced with dominant desire, his wide grip spanned my waist to pull me into his arms. Our lips met in a ravenous kiss, pent up anger fueling our lustful want for each other as he gripped the back of my thighs to lift me, my legs wrapping tightly around him. Winding my fingers through his hair, I pulled and tugged in desperation, his hands mirrored my actions in my tresses hanging down my back. I felt possessed, moaning into his mouth, sucking on his tongue. There was no concept of the bathroom we were in as we ravaged each other, completely engrossed in our deep, anger-fueled need to fuck each other senseless.

Turning towards the sink, Jackson secured me in his grip, his hand at my backside.

"I love your ass," he moaned. Setting me atop the counter, we struggled with needy hands and fingers, tugging and frantically pulling up my dress and pulling down my panties to reveal my nakedness beneath. His hands engulfed my slender waist as he pulled his lips from mine to attack my nipple, sucking it deep before swirling his tongue along the pebbled tip. I couldn't resist the urge to hold his head in place, my legs shaking amid the pounding tempo of my clenching body.

"Jackson!" I cried out in a breathless pant. He groaned through a final nibble, his husky breaths slipped through parted lips as he lifted me off the counter, making his way towards the wall. Pushing me against it, I yelped, barely able to catch up as he swiftly shoved his jeans down, his length bobbing against his stomach.

Bending, his large frame loomed against me, he spread my legs with his strong hands, "Is that what you want, little angel? You want me to fuck you? Maybe I should make you beg for it."

"Fuck..." I gasped, closing my eyes against the sheer decadence of his dominance.

"Is that a no? You don't think I should make you beg?" he questioned, sliding his fingers along my soaked core, gliding with ease.

"No!"

"Then tell me who you belong to," he ordered, his tone firm and sexy as he slid his fingers inside me, pressing deeply against my g-spot.

"You!" I screamed in absolute frustration and need, gripping his wrist in an attempt to push his fingers deeper, my body bowing with desire.

I was his. His, and his alone.

"You're fucking right, you do," he growled, pulling his fingers from my depths, moving between my widespread legs to thrust himself fluidly inside. He owned me in that moment—in every ridge, every ripple I felt against my sensitive nerves. I throbbed and pulsed around him. I would never tire of the feel of him. Never stop wanting him. Never stop loving him.

He pulled himself marginally from my core, plunging back inside as I mewled into his kiss. My hips met his thrusts measure for measure, needing him so deep inside me that I'd never survive otherwise. Our coupling was frenetic in our need for each other.

Pulling his lips from mine, he placed suckling kisses along my jaw, my collarbone. His hand slid beneath my back, pulling me upwards to arch my body towards him, my head falling back in abandon. I released a crazed whimper at the sensation, my body throbbing around his hardness, my climax imminent.

"Mmmm...yes, baby. You're so close. I want to feel you come around me. Fall for me." His words were my undoing. The sexy timber of his voice, combined with the steady tempo of his thrusts sent me plummeting over the precipice. I moaned his name in release as I slid my hands in his hair, gripping hard, riding the overwhelming waves of pleasure, convulsing uncontrollably. His thrusts pounded relentlessly as I rode the waves, in and out, deeper and deeper into my clutching depths, before he finally stilled against me and spilled his desire inside me as he released a delicious groan into my neck.

Harsh breaths amid the grasp of each other's arms, we

awaited the slowing of our rapid heartbeats in silence. Sliding himself out of me, he chuckled darkly at my elicited whimper. He slowly brought me back to the ground, steadying me when I wavered.

It took a minute. But then everything came crashing down around me. We'd had sex. Unprotected sex. In a bathroom while I was on my first date with another man. I was on birth control, but that was beside the point. I had no idea where he'd been the last two years.

He had a date out there waiting for him. Why had I done this?

He was playing with my broken heart, cruelly implying that all of the torture and heartache was nothing more than a temporary time break.

And I was letting him.

"I've got to get back to my date," I said stiffly as I pushed him away from me with all my might. After quickly yanking up my panties before pulling down my dress, I ran my fingers through my hair, skirted around him, and ran out of the bathroom back towards my booth, where Landry was still waiting. I needed to get out of here. I needed to get away from him.

"Everly, wait," he called after me, sounding pissed. He caught up to me before I got to the end of the hallway that led back into the dining area of the restaurant and grabbed my arm. "Leave me alone, Jackson," I pleaded with him, feeling like I was about to fall apart. I pulled away from him again and rushed to my table.

"I'm sorry. I need to leave." I rushed out an apology to Landry as he stood in alarm, his gaze ricocheting between me and Jackson who approached our table, his hair tousled and his clothes wrinkled from our session.

I turned for the door.

"Everly..."

"Let her go, Jackson," Landry growled at him.

"The hell I will," he spewed, quickly on my tail at the front doors. "Dammit, Everly, stop."

"Leave me the hell alone," I cried making my way to the curb to flag a taxi.

"Let me take you back."

"Are you serious?" I lashed out, spinning around to face him dead on, the motion throwing me off kilter. He reached to steady me, and I tore my arm from his supportive grip. "Don't. Touch. Me." The order was firm, and my eyes screamed a clear warning. Raising his hands in a sign of surrender, he backed away, his eyes a storm I could drown in.

"Whatever, Everly. That was a mistake anyway," he swore before striding back into the restaurant without a glance back.

An oncoming taxi pulled up to the curb.

I cried the whole way back to the dorm.

I was doomed to repeat the same mistakes over and over again.

Only News. Never Opinions.   19 Septembert

Dayton Valley News

Your Best Source of News Since 1965

Local Football Star Thriving on National Stage One Year After Twin's Accident.

Former South High Star Jackson Parker has hit the national stage one year after his twin brother's accident. Parker starred for Rutherford Academy's high school team before making the switch to their college roster this year. Rutherford Academy is consistently ranked #5 in the CBS polls, making Parker's starting position that much more impressive. Jackson Parker's brother, Caiden, was also a star at South High before his car accident last August. Caiden has been in a coma since that time.

"Parker's a real asset to our team," Rutherford Academy Head Coach Lynard Jones told us. "The fact that he's become a star on the national stage isn't a surprise after his debut season for us last year. Story Cont. A3.

Fire Destroys Five Homes. Cause Unknown.

Five homes were destroyed in a fire set by teenagers in the Richland Valley neighborhood last night.
Soty Cont. A9

12

THEN

Summer arrived, and somehow, I had found myself dating Caiden Parker.

Growing up, I'd thought about what it would be like to date one of them. It wasn't until later that those thoughts had grown into full-blown crushes...mostly aimed at Jackson.

It wasn't like I thought it would be.

He wasn't how I thought he would be.

He eased me into dating him. I didn't even really know it was happening until after.

At first, he was the Caiden that he'd always been...just more touchy-feely.

But something happened after those first couple of weeks. Somehow the desperation that had originally pushed me into the whole thing started to burrow its way into his heart.

That desperation became something dark...something ugly.

Something wrong.

CAIDEN PULLED up to the curb of my house and honked. My mother walked through the foyer in her bathrobe right at that moment, already drunk for the day.

"Where do you think you're going?" she grunted, slurring her words.

"Out," I responded succinctly.

"I don't think so—" she began, but I'd already opened the door and walked out, slamming the door on whatever she'd been about to say. She'd used and abused me for years but this last year, as the drinking had ramped up, she'd lost the ability to control me as much as she had before. I would probably suffer the consequences of what I'd just done when I got home.

But I wasn't going to worry about that right now.

Caiden got out of the Jeep and rounded the car to open the door for me. Before I could get in, he wrapped his arms around my waist and moved in to give me a kiss.

I couldn't help it. I flinched.

"What the fuck was that?" he asked, his voice coming out sharper than he'd ever used before with me. I hated the sound of his disappointment.

"It's just my mom. She didn't want me to come. Sorry, I know she's watching," I explained, and the anger on his face faded.

"Let's get to the lake. You can forget all about her there," he said softly, becoming the Caiden that I knew and loved.

I got into the Jeep and off we went. "Who all is going to be there?" I asked as Caiden drove out of my neighborhood.

"Just some guys from the team and a few of the girls they're interested in. That okay?"

"Yeah," I responded, already starting to dread the outing.

His teammates only put up with me because of him and Jackson.

Speaking of Jackson...

"Is your brother going to be there?" I asked, proud of myself for managing to keep my voice level.

It had been three weeks since he said anything other than hello to me. He hadn't hung out with us once, and if we were over at their house, he left immediately.

It was hell.

But this was what he wanted, right?

"Yeah, he's bringing the boat. I can't haul it in the Jeep. I think he's bringing a date," Caiden responded casually, and I was glad that he wasn't looking at me because just the thought of Jackson dating someone made me want to be sick.

I was a hypocritical bitch.

My stomach felt like it was full of rocks as Caiden pulled into the parking lot by the lake. Some of Caiden's teammates were loading a massive wakeboard boat into the water, and some people were already out on jet skis.

Just then, I heard a rumble and looked over to see Jackson pulling in to the parking lot in his truck, pulling the twin's parents' boat. Sure enough, Veronica Hollingsworth was perched in the seat next to him.

"Looks like Veronica's making strides," Caiden said with a laugh, unaware he was driving a knife into my heart.

I wanted to leave. But that was stupid. I waited for Caiden to walk around and open the door. As he helped me out, he made sure I slid down the front of him as I got out.

It made me feel a little sick inside.

What was wrong with me? Caiden was just as much of my best friend as Jackson was...or had been. Caiden was beautiful. He resembled some sort of dark prince with his tan skin, his almost black hair, and those dark, fathomless, brown eyes. Any girl would be lucky to have his attention. And I definitely had his attention. As he pulled his navy blue tank top off with one hand, like all hot guys seemed to have mastered, he showcased a pair of washboard abs that almost looked airbrushed, they were so perfect. Football definitely had blessed the Parker twins.

"Ready?" Caiden asked, holding out his hand for me to grab. I'd never felt more self-conscious as I walked hand in hand to where most of their friends were gathered.

Jackson expertly backed their boat into the water, and some of his teammates maneuvered it to be tied to the dock so it wouldn't float away while he was parking.

I couldn't not steal glances as Jackson parked the truck and walked over to the group with Veronica.

They were not holding hands.

Caiden let go of my hand and wrapped his arm around my waist. Jackson tracked the movement, a slight tick in his cheek. He looked at me just then for the first time since that day, and I had to hold in a gasp at the pain I saw in them.

I quickly looked away, unable to handle his emotions on top of my own.

Jackson slapped a few of his friends' hands and then headed to his and Caiden's boat without a word to us. Caiden seemed to deliberate for a moment before he started walking over, pulling me behind him.

"You don't want to ride with Kenneth?" I asked, my voice rising a little at the end, sounding hysterical to my ears.

Caiden looked at me, a calculated look in his eye. "I like our boat. And besides, I loaded snacks and drinks in there earlier, and with sober Jackson driving, I plan on taking advantage."

I felt a little desperate.

"You'll have to drive me home," I reminded him, for some reason not looking forward to a drunk Caiden, something I'd never had a problem with before.

Caiden swiped a kiss on my forehead. "I'll make sure to sober up before then," he said reassuringly.

Veronica frowned as I got into the boat, but quickly lost that frown when Caiden said hello to her. She wouldn't say anything nasty as long as the guys were around. I peeked at Jackson out of the corner of my eye as he gave a heavy sigh. Caiden walked over to him to help get out the life jackets.

Two more couples joined us, and away we went. The boat cut through the water and even with everything going on, I couldn't help but smile. It startled me when I realized that both Caiden and Jackson were watching me intensely, and my smile dropped. Jackson drove the boat out a little ways into a separate lagoon where we'd come many times before to swim and wakeboard. The water was calmer here, and not many other boats ventured in.

Jackson stood up and took off his t-shirt. And although Caiden's body was almost as impressive, my body had a much more intense reaction to the sight.

I had to suppress a groan, not even bothering to lie to myself that it wasn't from the sight of Jackson Parker's bare chest. My nipples beaded, brushing painfully against the thin cloth of my swimsuit. Why did he have to be freaking sexy? I followed the chiseled line of his jaw and the prominent muscles that I had the inane urge to lick...

I didn't stop drooling fast enough because once again, Jackson caught me looking at him. The pain present earlier had melted into heat. He looked at me like he wanted to eat me alive.

His reaction and my reaction to him just made me angry, so I stood up and bitterly yanked off my top, showcasing the cherry red bikini I'd found at Old Navy for a steal the week before.

Caiden was by my side in a flash. "I'm afraid you're going to get burnt, why don't you keep your shirt on?" he suggested, blocking me in so that no one else on the boat could really see me.

"I need to get a tan, and it's hot out. So I'm good," I responded, giving him a weird glance. He was chewing on his lip and almost looked mad.

"Do you not like my suit?" I asked, suddenly feeling self-conscious. He groaned and seemed to debate something in his head before he straightened up.

"Everything's good, babe," he said, taking a seat next to me and throwing his arm around my shoulders possessively. But the way he said it sounded like everything was not good.

We played around in the water for the next hour or so, taking turns wakeboarding while others swam in the shallower lagoon. Victoria didn't leave Jackson's side, and Jackson drove the boat the whole time so I made Caiden spend a lot of time swimming with me and one of the other couples. Dave and Lacey had been dating for the past year. Dave was one of Caiden's teammates that had never gone out of his way to be mean to me, and Lacy had always said hello to me in the halls, so I didn't mind hanging out with them.

"It's our turn," Caiden finally said, dragging me after him towards the boat. I usually loved to wakeboard, so it had kind of been killing me to avoid it all day. I hoisted myself onto the boat while Caiden swam out to where the board was floating.

After Caiden was on it, Jackson started the boat, and we watched Caiden do an assortment of tricks that I never in a million years could do. After Caiden rode for about twenty minutes straight, he finally crashed into the water, signaling that it was my turn.

I stepped onto the back steps of the boat that led into the water and slipped, banging the side of my foot onto one of the parts sticking out in the water and sending screaming pain throughout it.

"Crap," I hissed as I quickly sat down to take pressure off my now aching foot.

Caiden hadn't noticed that I fell, but Jackson was by my side in an instant, cradling my foot between his hands.

Suddenly, the pain didn't seem so bad.

"Careful," he warned, when I tried to move. "Let me just make sure it's not broken." I closed my eyes because he was too near. His warm mouth and the curves of his face and his unforgiving jaw make me feel slightly unhinged when he was this close. The pad of his thumb pressed to my skin. He stopped when I winced in pain, holding his hand there, waiting for me. He continued, and just the brush of his skin against mine awakened other things. Things I wasn't supposed to feel. My eyes opened of their own accord and locked with his. One of his hands moved to my face, his mouth slightly ajar as he looked at mine, both of us breathing quickly. I wanted him to kiss me. I wanted him to kiss me so badly that my blood started to sing, and all logic went rushing from my brain. It sat between us, quicksand that dragged us under so fast that fighting it seems impossible. He leaned toward me, for just a second, before his hands fell away suddenly, and he practically jumped backward.

"What's going on?" asked Caiden suspiciously as he swam up to us.

"I just fell," I explained guiltily. Had I really just almost kissed Jackson in front of everyone? What the fuck was wrong with me? "But I don't think I can board. My foot is killing me."

Caiden was still looking at Jackson. Caiden glared at Jackson like he...almost hated him.

"Can you help me back to my seat?" I asked, trying to interrupt whatever was going on between the twins.

"Sure," Caiden said sullenly, picking me up roughly suddenly and practically throwing me on one of the bench seats. He settled next to me, his hand possessively on my leg. He was holding me tightly, too tightly actually, and I moved my leg in discomfort. He squeezed tighter for a second more until I was sure that I was going to have bruises before he suddenly let go.

I stared at him shocked, but he was already in a conversation with one of the guys, his face lit up in a smile like nothing had happened.

I didn't say a word for the rest of the boat ride...and neither did Jackson.

WHEN WE GOT BACK on shore, it was time to start barbecuing. The group in the other boat had gotten back before us, and they'd already fired up the grills and started a game of sand volleyball.

My foot was feeling better, so I thought it would be fun to join the game. "Let's go play," I urged Caiden who usually loved sand volleyball.

He looked over to the group of his friends playing and frowned. "You should probably put your shirt back on to play," he commented.

"Why?" I asked with a frown, glancing over to where several of the girls were playing in just their bikinis. I'd slipped on my pair of faded denim shorts, so I would be more covered up than they were.

"Bikinis aren't for everyone..." he stated calmly. Shock crashed over me at his cruel words. Was he telling me that I didn't look good in my bathing suit? He'd had his hands all over me all day. A rush of embarrassment flooded over me. He'd acted like he loved my suit at their birthday party, but I guess that other one did cover more. Had Jackson been embarrassed to be seen with me all day, too?

Confidence had never been my strong suit, so when he handed me my shirt, not saying anything else, I put it on without a fight, not really wanting to play anymore.

I played a couple of rounds, but my heart wasn't really into it. When everyone walked over to the grills, I grabbed a single breast of chicken even though the burger was calling my name. I picked at my food while everyone stuffed themselves silly around me. Caiden chowed down on a burger, looking almost excited about what I'd chosen to eat.

"Sure you don't want a burger?" asked Jackson from two chairs down as he stared at my plate in confusion.

"I'm good," I told him, even as I cursed myself for my insecurities. I snuck a glance at Caiden, who laughed with some of his teammates. When he caught me studying him, he sent me a wink that didn't seem anywhere near as charming as it had in the past.

Jackson was quiet for the rest of the evening, and so was I.

It was going to be a long summer.

CAIDEN WAS at a special tight end training camp at the local college today, so I had a day to myself. I left early on my bike and set out for Target. Caiden had asked me to wait to go anywhere until he was done, but I wasn't about to do that.

While I pedaled, I thought about the night before. Caiden had gotten mad because I hadn't wanted to go beyond kissing. I'd started crying, and he'd apologized, but everything he'd said about me not loving him as much as he loved me stuck in my head.

I did love Caiden. I'd loved him since I was a little girl out on that playground. But something seemed to be warping that love as we dated. Caiden had started to be irrational, texting me every second about what I was doing and who I was with whenever we weren't together. When we were together, he spent most of that time criticizing me or cutting me down. This didn't feel like any good relationship that I'd ever heard of.

I parked my bike in the bike rack of the Target parking lot and locked it, not wanting to lose my mode of transportation. I grabbed a cart and began to peruse the aisles. I couldn't afford to buy anything really, but it was still fun to walk the aisles and see everything.

I turned the corner to head down the frame aisle, and suddenly, there was Jackson, staring at the selection.

Frozen in place, I debated what I should do. Jackson and I hadn't spoken since that awkward moment at the lake.

And I missed him. In spite of everything, I missed him.

I was about to run away like the coward I was when he spotted me.

"Eves?" he asked, like he couldn't believe I was there.

"Hey," I responded casually as I tried to pretend that I hadn't been about to run away from him.

"Are you here by yourself?"

"Yep," I replied, popping the P at the end as I wheeled my cart closer. I smiled when I saw Jackson's cart. There were at least five bags of the white chocolate Reese's in it along with a pack of Dr. Pepper. The boy had an addiction.

There was an awkward silence as we both just kind of stared at each other. "Looking for a frame?" I asked, and for some reason, the question made him blush.

"Uhh, yeah. Which do you like?" he said, gesturing to the selection.

"What's the picture of?"

His blush deepened. "Just of some people," he said in a rough voice.

Why was he acting so weird?

"Well, I think that white one would look good with any picture," I answered, picking the frame up and handing it to him. Our fingers brushed as he grabbed the frame and even that light touch sent tingles trembling across my skin.

I wanted him to touch me again. And again, and again, and again. Because each time he did, I forget that I live east and he lives west, and we'll never be together.

He quickly moved away from me like I'd burned him, and the withdrawal brought back the harsh, present state of our non-existent relationship. Our touches used to be an easy thing, as easy as breathing.

He put the frame in the cart, and then he hesitated like he was thinking hard. "Should we go look at the book aisle?" he asked, and my heart suddenly felt infinitely lighter. It was a thing we did. I had an obsession with books, and Jackson knew it. So every store we went to, I'd always dragged him to the book aisle to pick what I was going to read next. He'd bought me a Kindle for one of my birthdays, but there had always been something about holding an actual book in my hands that just did something for me.

"Let's go," I told him with a grin.

The Target book section wasn't large, but we must have

Heartbreak Prince

spent an hour going down the three aisles. He would tease me about some of the covers of the romance books that I liked, and I would roll my eyes and pretend to be offended. He picked up a cover of a Harlequin that had a Fabio like model on the front page and began to read a sex scene out loud, sending a poor old lady at the end of the aisle scrambling to run away from us.

I laughed until I cried.

Hours passed and somehow, we found ourselves at a café down the street, eating and talking like the last few weeks hadn't happened. I was faintly aware of my phone buzzing repeatedly, but I couldn't find it in myself to care enough to see who it was.

It was almost five when I finally looked at my phone and saw that Caiden had called me twenty-seven times.

"Crap," I said, looking at my phone.

"What's wrong?" Jackson asked, leaning towards me. We'd started lunch across the table from each other and ended up sitting next to each other on the guise of sharing a sundae. My heart had raced at an embarrassing pace as I watched him eat, and it reminded me about how firm his lips were when they'd first touched mine, and how they softened to enjoy every morsel of my mouth during that kiss.

"It's your brother. I hope nothing's wrong. He's called me over twenty times."

Jackson's eyes widened, and he pulled out his phone to check I guess if Caiden had called him as well. "He called me a bunch, too," he said worriedly.

I quickly pressed his name on my phone. It rang once, and Caiden picked up. "Where the fuck are you?" he barked sharply.

"Are you okay?" I asked, ignoring his tone.

"I went by your house to pick you up, and your mother

said you'd been gone all day. What have you been doing? Are you with him?"

"Am I with who?" I asked, my voice fading to a whisper as I cowered at his tone.

"My brother," he hissed.

I was quiet. "Yes, I am, Caiden. Why is that a problem?"

There was a long pause. Jackson tensed next to me as he listened to my conversation, there was no way not to hear since Caiden was yelling.

"Where are you? I'll come pick you up."

"I have my bike," I said crossly. "I think I'll just go home tonight."

Caiden's voice changed from anger to a cajoling tone. "LyLy, I'm sorry. Practice was just tough. I really want to see you. We can all hang out. Don't be mad."

I was still mad, but the chance to hang out with both of them and hopefully get things more back to they way they used to be was hard to pass up.

"Jackson and I are at East Bakery on Fifth Street," I told him.

"Be there in five," he said before abruptly hanging up.

"Let me guess. My brother wasn't pleased."

"No, he wasn't," I said, staring out the window. "He's been different lately. Have you noticed?"

"I've only noticed that he's barely speaking to me," Jackson said wryly. "Has he...been treating you all right?" he asked hesitantly.

I sighed and turned to look at him. "Maybe, I'm not sure I know how I'm supposed to be treated," I admitted.

Jackson opened his mouth to say something, but then Caiden was there, rushing through the door like we were in a burning building and he needed to save someone. A strange look passed over his face. That look that appeared whenever Jackson was in the vicinity. And then he wiped his face clean.

"There's my two people. Should we head back to the house and watch a movie? It's been a while, guys," he said jovially, as if we had just been busy and that was why we hadn't hung out.

"Sure, bro," Jackson responded, and there was a tightness in his tone and around his eyes.

Jackson threw my bike in the back of his truck, but of course, Caiden had me ride with him.

Caiden was deathly silent the entire way back. The tension was sky high and finally, I couldn't take it anymore.

"Why don't you go ahead and come out with it. I can feel how mad you are."

"And why would I be mad, Everly?" he asked, glancing at me blandly. "You don't have anything you need to tell me, do you?"

For a second, I wanted to tell him that I couldn't do this. Play the whole, "it's not you, it's me" card. Or tell him that I felt like it was ruining the friendship that we'd spent years building.

"Because if you knew how much I fucking cared about you, you would never want to hurt me," he suddenly said. And the words died in my throat.

"Everything's good, Caiden," I told him with a false smile, my heart beginning to bleed inside of me. "I would never want to hurt you."

And that was the truth. Caiden and Jackson were as important to me as air.

We pulled into the twin's massive driveway, and Caiden made sure to hold my hand as we walked towards the back entrance and passed by Jackson's truck. We all ended up in the media room in their house, a place I'd been to a million times in the past.

But unlike all those times, the mood in the room was angry, suspicious...and heartbroken. And I wasn't sure which of us was feeling what emotion.

We ended up falling asleep during the first movie, one of the Jason Bourne movies. I woke up to a dark room, the screen showed the credits and cast a faint glow over the boys asleep in bean bags next to me.

This was a thing we'd always done. Sleepovers with the three of us. But right now, lying next to Jackson in the darkened room, sleep evaded me. I listened to his steady breaths, relishing in the familiar sound.

Yearning was a feeling I was familiar with, or should I say, being left yearning. My life had been filled with a deep desire to have more, to be more. But Jackson had woken up something inside of me that I never thought I would experience.

I lightly slid my fingers along his arm. The light from the television highlighted his beautiful, masculine face in his serene slumber, and I admired every perfect detail.

I'm so fucked, I thought to myself, before succumbing to a sleep filled with anxious dreams.

13

NOW

Jackson

"One of the strawberry cupcakes, please," I said as I pointed to one of the pink, frosted confections on the third shelf. The employee grabbed the cupcake and boxed it up, trying to flutter her eyelashes seductively as she did so. Someone needed to get her a mirror pronto so she could see how ridiculous she looked. Besides, she was blonde. And I didn't do blondes.

I took the cupcake and walked to my truck. And then I just sat there. I stared at the cupcake, and for one moment...I allowed myself to feel. And to remember.

I remembered Everly's face the first time Caiden and I had shown up with a box of cupcakes. How she'd cried because she was so happy. Caiden and I had felt like idiots for not doing something bigger but she'd made it seem like we'd given her a priceless gift. Every year after that we'd brought her some. It had become a contest of sorts eventually, who would pick up the cupcakes first. Until finally we'd just started buying our own to give her. It was a little tragic looking back now at all the signs I should have caught about my brother and his feelings for Everly.

I let myself remember for one more moment about how Everly looked when we'd sang *Happy Birthday* to her, how the light from the solitary candle had reflected off her gold hair, making her look like an angel.

My little angel.

When my moment was up, I pushed the memories away, locking them up tight where I wouldn't have to see them, and then I threw the cupcake out my truck window, not caring what it hit.

Happy Birthday, Everly.

Everly

"Do you really think this is a good idea?" Lane murmured as we approached the entrance to the events room. Of course, Rutherford wouldn't have their big Halloween dance in a smelly gymnasium. Instead, it was outfitted with a room that was basically a large ballroom, which they called an "events room" to sound less snotty.

It didn't work.

My mouth fell open as I looked around at the way the enormous room had been transformed to resemble a high-class club you could walk into in New York City or Vegas. "Is this real life?" I muttered, looking around at the lounge seating placed strategically around the room, the bars and food stations set up against the north and south walls, and the large dance floor with a stage set up in the middle of it where a DJ was currently spinning a remix of Taylor Swift's "Delicate" that immediately made me want to wade into the already busy crowd and start dancing.

"Just wait until the end of year dance," Lane responded, looking around the room unimpressed. "This will look like kid's play compared to that. Maybe we should just wait for that?"

Lane had wanted to come to the Halloween dance, and it just showed how good of a friend she was that she was begging to leave before something terrible happened. This was my first school event, but my first shower at this school had included snakes, so I didn't have high expectations. Everything had been uneasily quiet over the last couple of weeks and I was hoping the trend would continue tonight. *My birthday was especially quiet.* Instead of the cupcake the twins used to bring me each year, I'd eaten a cookie from the cafeteria by myself.

"We'll be fine. There's a million staff members here watching everything," I responded.

Even if I shouldn't, I looked around for him, my heart beating wildly at the just the idea of seeing him all dressed up.

I'd worn a daring red dress that I'd found in a second-hand shop a few weeks earlier with a small black masquerade mask that somehow made me feel hidden, even though it only covered my eyes. All I could think when I saw the dress was how Jackson always loved me in red. I should have bought the black one that had been next to it, because Jackson would know that I'd worn this dress for him the second he saw me.

But trying to please him was one of those habits that I'd

probably be trying to break for the rest of my life. They needed a twelve-step program for getting over Jackson Parker because no matter how much he tortured me...I always wanted him. The events of my ruined date with Landry had only made it worse. It was a strange thing that you could hate yourself, and love someone else so much.

I let out a big breath when I didn't see him anywhere, not examining too closely whether it was one of relief or disappointment as we waded through the crowd to get a drink.

The bartender was only half-heartedly carding, and he just winked at me when I showed him my fake ID, handing me a Red Bull and vodka along with his number written on the cocktail napkin he wrapped around the drink.

I threw out a thanks, my spirits a little bit lifted that I wouldn't have to endure the night completely sober, and pulled Lane over to the dance floor where we began to dance on the fringes of the crowd as the DJ played hit after hit.

Lane yelled over the noise that the DJ was actually one of those really famous ones that always worked clubs for celebrity events, and I nodded, only mildly impressed. There was a haunted house in the next building over that Lane said we would go to after we had a few drinks. Because evidently, it made everything seem scarier.

I was a few songs in when I saw him. He was sitting in the corner in one of the lounge areas, surrounded by a crowd of people all desperate to talk to him. There was a girl perched on his lap, a different one than from the night of my ruined date. A brunette this time.

Jackson was stunning in a fitted black suit, the lines hugging his tight, muscled frame. Blue eyes, white shirt, slim black tie, and I was speechless—caught off guard by the herd of elephants galloping in my chest. He was devastating, as each woman here could testify to, including me.

I couldn't seem to look away as he interacted with everyone around him. But weirdly enough, it didn't seem like they were people to him. They were vessels to use. And just as bad, they viewed him the same way. He wasn't Jackson, the complicated, irreverent, talented man that I'd been in love with for half my life. He was a celebrity at Rutherford — someone they could brag about hanging with when they went out partying with their friends the next night. A status symbol, not unlike a Lamborghini or a pair of Christian Louboutin shoes. I stopped dancing and stood like a statue and watched it all.

I suddenly felt woefully naïve and unprepared to be in the same place as Jackson Parker. The same sort of naïve and stupid I'd been the last time with him and Caiden.

How many times did I have to put myself in situations like this before I learned?

"Let's go do some shots and then head to the haunted house," I yelled over the noise at Lane, suddenly not feeling like dancing anymore. She was looking over at Jackson too and gave me a thumbs up. I'd told her about what had happened on my ruined date with Landry, and she was firmly in the "keep Everly James away from all things Jackson Parker" camp.

After grabbing a few shots, we left the room. I snuck one more look over my shoulder, but he was still wrapped in the loyal followers around him. It didn't seem like he had seen me.

Lane had to hold onto me as we walked because her heels were so high. I'd been bitter about not being able to wear cute heels to go with my dress, but the thought of walking through a haunted house in heels made me glad that I had on my flats.

The haunted house was set up in the indoor facility of the football team. Volunteers from the school and outside performers were brought in to run it. I'd never been a big fan of haunted houses...the whole scared of the dark thing, but Lane had promised me that it wasn't bad. It was more of a "fun" haunted house then a scary one...whatever that meant.

Some of the hockey team was ahead of us, Landry included. We'd exchanged a few texts since our terrible date when I'd snuck off and ended up fucking Jackson in the bathroom...and he'd been surprisingly sweet. We hadn't talked exactly about what had gone down, but there was no way that he didn't know. Every time I thought of it, thick shame overwhelmed my entire body.

This messed up thing between Jackson and I didn't just affect us, it trickled down to everyone around us, and I wondered when the casualties would be enough.

I made Lane stay back so that the hockey team didn't notice our approach. It was one thing to talk to Landry on the phone, but I wasn't quite ready to have to face him yet. I could be brave like that another time.

"I don't think he's done with you," she said as we stood there. "How could he be?"

I groaned. I literally left the table and ended up on the bathroom sinks with another guy. "He should hate me."

"Don't be so hard on yourself," she chided gently, socking me softly in the arm. "Landry would be a fool if he somehow missed that something was going on between you and Jackson. It's so obvious that it's practically pasted to both of your foreheads."

I snorted and smiled fondly at my friend. Lane was

dressed in some kind of Victorian, black, lacy dress with black stilettos and had been getting looks all night. The girl had style. I really needed her to teach me her ways.

"They're inside," Lane squealed as she started to drag me towards the entrance where two people in Grim Reaper costumes manned the doors. They didn't say anything, and I couldn't see their faces, but it felt like they were staring hard at me. Unease slid down my neck.

We walked inside, and I immediately had an iron grip on Lane's arm. It was freaking dark, and I started to sweat as I thought about the snake and being trapped in that cellar. This was the worst idea in the history of the world.

A killer clown jumped out from the shadows, and we both shrieked. My voice was going to be hoarse after this. We waded through a room set up to resemble a prison cell. Screaming prisoners reached out for us as a guy with an axe sticking out of his head jumped out from behind us. Another room held a bloody operation room, complete with someone lying on a stretcher missing half their body and random body parts littered around the room. There was a mad scientist room, a vampire room, a room made up of crazy mirrors. On and on it went. Lane seemed like she was having the time of her life next to me, but I was about to start running.

I stopped short when we entered a room designed to look like it was filled with snakes. There were cages set up along all of the walls with hopefully fake snakes on them. Lights cast snake images on the floor and there was a hissing sound playing through the speakers.

I screamed as something slid beside my ankles. The lights that were dimly lighting the room all of a sudden clicked off ,casting us in darkness. It was like someone had decided to combine my two worst fears in one room.

"Lane," I squeaked, reaching out for her. I caught a piece of her clothing and moved closer to her.

Suddenly, a breath on my ear whispered, "I'm not Lane." Then a hand was clasped over my mouth, and I was dragged backward.

I started kicking and crying but the sounds coming out of my mouth were muffled, and the hissing sounds covered everything else. I was dragged into a dark tunnel, and then there were what felt like a million hands pulling at me in the darkness.

"Killer."

"Slut."

"Cunt."

"Bitch," the voices cried. Over and over, until I felt like I was going mad.

All of a sudden, the hands pushed me forward and I fell through the side of the tunnel, onto my face and into the exit of the set-up. The hockey players had just come out, and I scared them probably even more than what they'd just gone through by appearing suddenly out of nowhere.

I was screaming and crying and looking around for anyone I knew. Landry was there all of a sudden, coming from the back of the group. He picked me up and called for someone to call 911.

Lane dashed out of the exit just then, a panicked look on her face. "Everly!" she cried. "What happened?"

"Someone grabbed me," I sobbed. "Someone at this school is after me." I buried my head in Landry's neck, and I heard him asking Lane what I was talking about. Landry carried me out of the indoor facility into the cool night air, and I began to catch my breath. My heart was still beating out of my chest, and I was sure there were bruises on both knees from where I'd been pushed.

I stood there huddled against Landry while Lane fluttered around me until a squad car pulled up. A cop strode towards us. He had a crisp navy uniform that unfortunately for him looked to be at least a size too small, judging by the way his belly bulged above his belt. His partner, a severe-looking female cop followed after him. "Are you the ones that called 911?" the male cop asked. The three of us nodded, and I pulled myself away from Landry. The cold and the adrenaline were making me shiver.

"Someone attacked me in there," I told him shakily. "They pulled me out of one of the rooms, and then there were people touching me and yelling things at me. And then finally, they threw me out here."

The two cops looked at each other. My story sounded crazy, but surely they thought it was too crazy for someone to make up.

The woman cop came up to me. "What's your name, sweetheart?" she asked kindly. "I'm Officer Wilson."

"Everly James," I responded in a choked voice.

"Your last name is James?" the overweight cop asked, and just by the way he said it, I knew what he had to be thinking. James might be a common name around the country, but in this state, it only made people think of one thing.

"Yes," I responded curtly.

Officer Wilson cleared her throat.

"There's been someone after her since she came to this school," interjected Lane. "Someone put a snake in the bathroom and locked her in one of the building's cellars. She has some kind of stalker."

"Hmmmm," Officer Wilson said with a frown. She pulled out a notepad and started to write something down, but I could tell by her partner's body language that as soon as he'd heard my last name, any hope I'd had for getting help was going to be gone.

"Well, we will look into this and get back to you," he said, taking a step away.

"Don't you need her contact information?" snapped Landry, sounding angry on my behalf.

The male cop flushed in anger at Landry's tone, but Officer Wilson did step forward to take my information.

I didn't feel any better after they left.

"You're sleeping in my room tonight," said Lane, rubbing my back and giving everyone who had gathered around us to watch a dirty look. "You guys are all fucking twisted," she yelled out as she stared everyone down, like she was trying to find out who the culprits were.

"Let's just go," I whispered, my voice feeling scratchy from all the screaming I'd done. I looked at Landry, who was standing there, gazing at me with something that looked a lot like longing.

"Thanks for letting me freak out all over you," I told him awkwardly. I couldn't look at Landry without thinking about the other night.

"Anytime, Everly. And you still owe me a full date," he said charmingly. My mouth dropped open at that. Maybe he was crazy. Or just enjoyed pain. Because that was all he was going to get by spending time with me. "Do you guys need a ride?"

"Are you parked in the athletic parking lot? Because that's about as far as our dorm is," answered Lane, and he nodded.

"True."

"See you later, Landry," I told him, giving him a hug. He pulled me close to him and buried his face in my hair. I swore he took a big inhale. It was a little bit uncomfortable when I pulled away from him, and now his cheeks were flushed.

Lane luckily took control of the situation and pulled me away to walk back to our dorms.

I shook as we walked. I hated feeling out of control of my life, and that was the very description of my time since coming here. Lane began to discuss various people she suspected it could be, and I didn't recognize anyone she named. Surely it was someone that I'd met at some point. Except really...there was only a handful of people I knew at this school.

I looked back just then, something calling me. And I knew even before I saw him who it was.

Jackson.

He stood in the entryway of where the dance was being held, and he just watched me. Catching me in his stare, he lifted two fingers and brought them to his lips, sending me a kiss that felt more like a warning.

I didn't have anything I could say in return.

I was too tired of playing a game that I didn't know all the rules to.

I was too tired of nursing a bleeding heart.

14

THEN

They said that time healed all wounds, but two months had passed, and I hadn't found that to be the case. I missed Jackson. I missed everything about him. I played our history on repeat through my useless brain—sledding on a snowy winter day, pizza on Fridays, the warmth of his fingers as he held my hand, lazy Sundays, racing in the pool, the stubborn set of his jaw, but most of all, the brilliant smile that that touched me like a bright star in the darkest part of a midnight sky and that I suspected he kept just for me.

I didn't have a chance to love Caiden the way he wanted, because his brother had stolen my heart who knew how long before.

It made me a monster, but I couldn't help myself. I didn't want to.

THERE WAS A PARTY TONIGHT. I'd never been one for social events, but Caiden had been *on* a tear this summer. He'd accepted every invitation he'd been given—there were about a million of them—and I had started to get the sneaking suspicion that he was doing it just to show me off. Inevitably, Jackson would show up at some point, Victoria on his arm, and then the night would be even more miserable.

I couldn't wait for school to start. It was amazing that I'd been dreading this next year so much since the guys would be at their new school. Things had changed so much, and for someone who didn't like change to begin with, I was having a lot of trouble coping with it all.

I'd lost two best friends the day that I'd started dating Caiden and it was funny that even at a crowded party, I somehow felt more alone than ever.

"Can you stop looking so fucking depressed, Everly?" snapped Caiden as we walked to the bonfire. I cringed at his tone. It was how he talked to me almost all the time now. Nothing I did was right to him. I stopped in my tracks, sick to death of feeling this way.

"If you don't like it so much, Caiden, we can be done," I hissed at him.

He moved fast, pinning me against a tree with the weight of his body. He grabbed my chin with one hand, gripping it so hard, I knew it would leave a bruise. He'd been doing that a lot lately, but never as aggressively as this.

"Listen here, you little bitch. We're never going to be done. The sooner you accept that, the sooner things will be easier for you."

I was shaking, and he seemed to like that because he pressed against me even closer, until my back was digging against the tree. "Caiden...why?" I whispered.

"You just don't understand how much I love you," he told me, his voice coming out pained and raw.

If this was love, it was the dirty and flawed form of it that ruined people's souls. It wasn't a love that I would wish on anyone else.

"Are you going to behave?" he asked, and I nodded stiffly, sure my anger shone in my eyes. "LyLy," he said, his voice changing to sweet so suddenly that it gave me whiplash. "I don't want it to be like this. You don't have to make it so difficult."

I said nothing, and he sighed before pushing me hard against the tree for good measure, snapping my head against the bark. I gritted my teeth from the pain, aware he would get even angrier if I cried. "Come on," he ordered, before grabbing my hand and dragging me towards the bonfire crowded with people that I wanted no part of.

I stood there as Caiden courted his loyal followers, numb inside, lost, and afraid.

And then I saw him.

He was standing across the fire from me. Victoria was hanging off of him while she talked to someone, but his eyes were on me. Only on me.

Kiss my soul, my eyes begged.

I want to, his answered back.

"I'll be right back," I whispered to Caiden, but I didn't even pay attention if he heard me, I just walked away. Even without looking, I knew Jackson followed.

He met me in the glen right behind the party. A new song started. I recognized it instantly. It was "Chasing Cars," an odd choice for a party to be sure.

He stared at me, and I was undone. The violins came in, then the piano, and then the slow and sure beating of a drum.

And in that moment, I thought I loved him.

And in that moment, I thought I might want to marry him someday.

And the music built, and our hands met.

And I looked up into his soft blue eyes, and I cried.

Fight for me. Want me. I whispered to him without saying any actual words.

His lips collided against mine, devouring me, hard and strong. His tongue plunged past my lips, and I took him in, kissing him back with everything I had. His body sank against mine, melting into me. He twisted his fingers roughly through the strands of my hair and his other hand —oh fuck, his other hand slid up the bare skin of my leg and gripped my ass through my shorts, pulling me harder against him. The pressure between my thighs tightened, and I could feel the hardness of him perfectly aligned with me– just his old, faded blue jeans and the thin material of my shorts keeping us apart.

And I didn't want to stop him.

I wanted him. I wanted that boy more than anything in the world.

I'D SPENT the entire night stunned that it happened, pressing my fingers to my lips to recapture the feeling of it. His mouth was as soft and pliant as I'd remembered. And then he deepened the kiss. He sought it out like he needed to own my every breath. Groaning low in his throat and pulling me tight against him, he kissed me hard, like it was something he'd wanted for a long, long time. It was a perfect kiss—a life-altering kiss.

Even now, my fingers kept going to my lips, trying to

recapture it. He left and returned to the party. He couldn't even look at me.

And it didn't matter because now I knew for sure, whether or not he'd admit it, some part of him wanted this too.

I had to end it with Caiden.

I WAITED until Caiden dropped me off, too afraid to do it in person after what had happened earlier. My hands were shaking as I picked up my phone. I was ugly inside, selfish, worthless...the worst kind of human. But I couldn't do it anymore.

"Caiden, I can't be with you," I told him in a choked voice as soon as he picked up. I was such a coward for doing this over the phone. "It's changing you into something I don't even recognize. I just think we need to go back to being friends. It's what's best for both of us."

There was just silence on the other end of the phone. His breath echoed down the line in short, tempered pants. Then a wounded sound came out of him, like he was a dying animal, and I never wanted to hear that sound again. I hated this. I hated hurting him. But I hated *us* more.

"You can't do this," he said brokenly.

"We're done," I told him woodenly, even as all the pieces of me that Caiden owned since I met him chipped away.

And I realized that I felt free.

15

NOW

Jackson

I hadn't slept in what seemed like days. When I'd finally fallen asleep last night—thanks to some sleeping pills—I found myself trapped in nightmares starring Caiden. In my dream, he just stared at me, his eyes dead, only for pieces of him to shatter and disappear right in front of me.

So, now I was here. Sitting beside Caiden's bed, staring at the person I'd destroyed.

I didn't come here often. It was too hard. My parents urged me to visit him, saying that he could hear me when I spoke and we needed to be there for him, but I left all that to them.

I was the last person Caiden would want to hear from.

The clock ticked loudly on the wall. My exhaustion was bone-deep. But it wasn't just physical.

I was so tired of hating Everly, and for hating myself for the fact that I'd been in love with a girl almost my whole life.

The fun of this push-pull between us since she'd reappeared had quickly faded. And now I just felt a hollow ache.

"I don't think I can stop myself, brother," I whispered hoarsely as I stared at him.

Would you ever have forgiven me? I wondered in my head, not able to say the words out loud.

I swear, a voice inside my head answered, *No*.

Sighing, I stood up to leave, taking one last look at my twin. His motionless form represented years of guilt.

"I can't do it anymore," I told him quietly.

At least I could console myself that I wouldn't have to face my brother in hell.

That place would be reserved for me and my sins.

Everly

This school was ruined for me. Monsters were everywhere. Every student was a suspect, and I constantly looked behind me to see if someone was following me.

And I was pretty sure it was all because of *him*.

Which was why today, I, Everly James, had decided to stop being Jackson Parker's doormat, and I was going to confront him.

I texted him after class.

We need to meet.

The three dots on my phone told me he'd seen my message, and I waited anxiously for him to answer back.

I'm intrigued.

What an insufferable prick, I thought as I read his response.

E: Meet me in the library at 7.

J: No, let's meet by the lake.

E: I'm only meeting you in a public place, asshole.

J: Scared?

Scared. The word taunted me. I hated how easily he baited me, but last time I'd tried to meet him somewhere I'd ended up in a cellar. There was no way I was making that mistake again.

Library only.

There was another long pause as I waited for him to respond.

Meet you in the stacks on floor 6.

I could do this. I could end whatever this was once and for all. I could stop fearing what life would be like if Jackson Parker wasn't there.

HE WAS WAITING for me when I arrived, already set up in a table far too secluded for my liking. Since I was new here, I hadn't realized that level six of the stacks were ones that were underground. There were study tables set up here and there, but only the most serious of students would come down here. It was seriously creepy. I was tempted to run for the hills, but the look on his face was so sullen, I couldn't stop myself from continuing to walk towards him.

"Hi," he said quietly.

My hands were shaking as I stood there in front of him. "Were you behind the snake, and the cellar, and the haunted house on Halloween?" I blurted out.

He just stared at me woodenly. There was no way to read his face. And maybe that should have been answer enough, but you never could tell with Jackson.

I grabbed the front of his flannel, a flannel I suddenly recognized was the one that had been in my room, and that I'd worn, just a few weeks ago. The sight infuriated me...even if it was originally his.

"Answer me, you asshole," I seethed as I pulled at him. "I know you hate me. I know that I'm the worst person in the world to you. But I can't take it anymore. You've won. I give up," I gasped brokenly, all of my anger fading into abject loneliness and despair.

He shook his head a fraction and said, "Everly." That one word lived within me as a shiver. This pull, the draw I felt toward him, it killed me.

It had never happened before with anyone else. I couldn't figure out why it was still there, why it was always him.

Then it hit me. I wasn't alone, everyone had this reaction. Few people possessed the type of magnetism that cast a spell, yet he had it in spades. I didn't stand a chance to fight off his magic.

But I wanted to so fucking bad.

"Tell me what you want from me," I begged. "I just want this thing, this awful thing between us, to be over."

"What I want is to stop missing you," he groaned, his eyes filled with confused anguish.

"What does that mean? I'm right here. I've always been right here," I told him, even as tears streamed down my face.

Before I knew it, he grabbed me around my waist and slammed my ass down hard against the study table we'd been standing by and positioned his body between my legs. I quickly leaned back to get away from him, and with the momentum of my movements, we both fell against the table, his body crashing on top of mine.

"Get off of me! I hate you," I screamed, throwing out my arms, trying to find purchase.

Slowly, he leaned up on both his arms, his chest rising and falling fast as he hovered over me. I was trapped between both his arms and weighed down by the heaviness of his body that had fallen perfectly between my thighs. I tried to wrench my body and twist my way free, wiggling between the hard length of him and the cold, wooden table.

"Stop. Stop...just stop fucking wiggling like that under me, Everly," he whispered as he locked his gaze to mine. A strange burn spread across my chest and heated my cheeks as our eyes, less than an inch away from each other, stared into one another's. Both of our bodies turned stiff and rigid.

"Everly," he whispered my name again. The way it fell from his lips sounded like a prayer or a wish.

My head spun, and my heart fluttered with the ache of pressure that was building against his body between my legs. He searched my face, my eyes, my lips, my cheeks—

like he was looking for me, but couldn't quite find me. "You don't hate me."

"Yes. I. Do." I insisted.

He slid his body against mine, and I tried not to move, but the feel of him made me throb and tingle everywhere I had skin—which was of course, all over. My heartbeat pounded in my ears, and the warm heat from his mouth as it landed against my skin made me want to move my body along his.

This wouldn't happen again. I'd been caught in this never-ending cycle that only led to me hating myself. I wouldn't do it anymore.

"Jackson," I whispered. "I'm done. I'm so fucking done."

"Don't say that," he ordered.

"Get off me. *Now!*"

He gazed at me for a long moment before he finally slid off me. He seemed confused, conflicted even.

The resolution I'd been desperate for was growing. Suddenly, the determination to make this break once and for all flooded me. He had punished me enough, how I felt about myself was plenty of torture by itself. But I wouldn't let him do this to me anymore.

I couldn't.

"Everly," he said again, like I was being unreasonable.

"We are done," I told him calmly. "If you see me, I want you to go the other way. I never want to have to talk to you again."

He stared at me like I was talking crazy, like he couldn't believe the words that were actually coming out of my mouth. And why should he? I'd been running after him for years. It was always me taking the steps towards him that we should have been taking together.

Well, not anymore.

"I'm going to leave this room, and I don't want you to follow me. Do you understand?"

He looked lost standing there, almost like a little kid.

"Goodbye, Jackson," I whispered.

I left the room, leaving my heart behind. I couldn't take it with me, it would always belong to him.

16

THEN

It was raining.

And I was the stupid girl who'd biked through the rain to the house of the brother of the guy I'd just broken up with. I sat in the driveway, the rain beating on my shoulders as I wondered what in the hell I was doing.

But this yearning inside of me, this need to see him. I couldn't get rid of it.

I didn't want to get rid of it.

Caiden had told me Jackson had moved into the pool house this summer, so I didn't even have to worry about seeing Caiden as I passed through the gate into the backyard.

I took a deep breath, and then I knocked. When he didn't immediately open the door, my mind began to run wild. Was he on a date? Was there a girl inside there with him right then? Was I too late?

My thoughts flew away when he finally opened the door to me standing there, looking like a drowned rat.

"Everly?" he asked, looking confused to see me there. His confusion turned to worry. "Is everything okay?"

"I broke up with him," I whispered.

There was only silence as he stared at me.

Then his lips were suddenly on mine, and it was like the entire fabric of the universe had been torn asunder. Stars were shooting, clouds were billowing, wind was swirling, water was falling, the planets were aligning and realigning.

He kissed my top lip gently, then my bottom one, and finally his tongue slipped along them both. My own tongue slid out to meet his. He pressed his lips more firmly against mine, and he entered my mouth, all dark velvet. My heart was wrenched from its moorings, and the pain was so intense, I nearly cried out. But instead, I grabbed his shoulders in a futile effort to ground myself somehow, because I was pretty sure I had just launched into the stratosphere and I was terrified.

I didn't know how I'd ever live in the normal world again.

He pulled away from me slowly and then led me inside and shut the door behind us. Immediately, we were encased in silence. "Why don't you take a shower and get warm? You look like you're freezing to death," he commented in a hoarse voice.

Right. I was standing here dripping wet. And we needed to slow down. What were we even doing?

I nodded, and walked to the bathroom, closed the door and started the shower. Steam started to fill the room as the water heated up. Nerves crept in while I showered. He wanted me right? That kiss was a good sign, wasn't it?

I got out of the shower, realizing that I hadn't brought in any of Jackson's sweats to change into. My clothes were soaked, and I didn't relish the thought of putting them back on. I wrapped one of his big, fluffy white towels around me and cracked open the door. Jackson was sitting on the edge of his bed, staring at the floor.

I took a deep breath and walked out. He immediately looked up at me. His eyes were hot and heavy on my skin.

And then I found myself letting the towel wrapped around me fall heavily in a damp heap around my feet. My heart thudded wildly in my chest as he looked everywhere at me, devouring me, and I shuddered with the need for him to touch me.

My eyes squeezed shut tightly, too scared and too terrified that he wouldn't like what he saw. I'd never been naked in front of a guy before. And this was Jackson.

A few seconds later, I felt something in the room shift—it was like the air became thicker and hotter. Blinking my eyes open, Jackson was standing next to me, so close, the warmth of his body made my cool skin prickle up with goosebumps. I stopped breathing. I forgot my own name. I didn't know how to move. My cheeks flooded with warmth, and my scalp tingled with heat, and a throb began building between my legs, pounding like it was my heartbeat.

I was still too frightened to look into his eyes, so I stared at his neck and watched it hammer with the pulse of his heart. I watched the rise and fall of his chest as it quickened. Rise and fall. Faster and Faster.

What was I supposed to do now? I'd never felt this much. The emotions, the need, the want—it was overwhelming. The rise and fall of his chest became even faster. Then he stepped closer, lifting my chin to look at him. Taking one more step closer, he backed me up against his dresser. Sliding his hands up over my neck and grabbing a handful of my wet hair, he leaned down and opened his mouth over mine. When our lips touched, my body went liquid. I thought my bones and muscles were going to melt into a thick, hot mass on the floor.

"Everly," he whispered against my lips. "Do you want me to stop?" he asked, slowly skating his fingertips over my shoulders and collarbone.

"No," I whispered back hoarsely. "Don't stop. Don't ever stop."

"I've wanted you forever," he whispered as the heat of his warm breath brushed over my lips. There were no more words. When our lips touched again, there was more urgency, an uncontrollable need. His breath hitched as our tongues tangled together, and my hands were grasping at his shirt, clumsily lifting it over his head. I slid my hands to his waist, unbuttoned his jeans, lowered his zipper, and let everything that was keeping us apart fall to the floor. He kicked at his jeans, sending them flying across the room to land in a crumpled heap on his bed. His fingers hesitantly curled around the weight of my breasts, caressing the rough pads of his fingers over my sensitive skin, touching, then tasting, licking, sucking.

My pulse crashed in waves. I'd known nothing in my life with such certainty as the fact that what happened right now was all I was capable of wanting, that nothing in the world mattered more to me.

He hissed when I reached down and took him in my hand. Gripping him firmly, I marveled as the smooth, taut skin throbbed and pulsed under my touch. Slowly, I moved my fist, sliding it up and down. Wrapping his hands around the back of my neck and kissing me deeper, he thrust himself against the palm of my hand, moaning into my mouth. Still wrapped around each other, we stumbled awkwardly to his bed, falling over the covers, laughing into each other. I was positive he had to feel the hammering of my heart as his hands and lips roamed my entire body. My head spun in circles.

Jackson was so utterly beautiful, it nearly broke my heart, my very own golden prince in living color. I gripped the blankets that surrounded us as I watched him run his lips over me. When he reached the insides of my thighs, his light, silky hair brushed along my skin, sending shock waves through my body.

A low moan escaped my lips, and his mouth was on me, fingers inside me, as I frantically pressed myself against him, unable to control my hunger. "Jackson," I whimpered, pulling him up. His eyes were glazed over, a delirious smile on his face, lips glistening from me.

"I'm never going to get enough of you, Everly," he said, looking into my eyes. "Even when we're old and gray and the entirety of our lives are nothing but memories, I will never get enough of you."

He captured my lips with his as I wrapped my legs around him. He lifted his lips from mine; his cheeks turned red with the question in his eyes. I nodded and smiled, my cheeks burning to probably match the color of his. He wildly grabbed at his pants that were on the covers next to us and pulled a foiled wrapper out of one of the pockets. I yanked it out of his hand and ripped it open. "Let me," I whispered.

And as he held himself over me, I slowly rolled it over the length of him with shaky fingers. When I was done, he leaned his forehead against mine, gently laid himself over me, and grasped both my hands with his.

Pulling them over my head, he entwined our fingers together, "Tell me what you want, Everly."

"All I ever wanted was you, Jackson," I whispered, lifting my hips to meet his.

"Then, I'm yours," he breathed, sliding slowly inside me. I gasped as he pushed past my barrier and sharp pain struck me. His forehead lifted off mine, our eyes locked, and the way he looked at me completely stole the air from my lungs. I would never feel this way about anyone else in my life.

His mouth claimed mine as we moved together. No, it was more than my mouth he claimed. He claimed my body, my soul, my mind—he claimed all of me. I knew without a single doubt in my heart, I would never love another person as completely as I loved Jackson Parker. We slowly healed from the tragedy of the summer, wrapped in each other's arms. Nothing else mattered, nothing but this.

The heat from his body up against mine, the smell of the shampoo he used, the press of his lips against mine, and there was nothing and no one else in the world, but us.

The words of Lewis Carroll murmured in my mind, "In another moment, down went Alice after it, never once considering how in the world she was to get out again."

We lost ourselves together—our hearts were crashing and pounding together like a thunderstorm beneath our chests.

It was only after, when we were wrapped in each other's arms, that reality hit.

"I'll ruin us," Jackson whispered to me in the dark, his voice a confession like I was the redemption for his rotten soul.

"I won't let you," I swore fiercely, even as my mind drifted to Caiden and the promises I'd made to him.

"Promise me." Jackson's voice was urgent, his voice fierce.

I couldn't shake the apprehension I felt. It was littered through my body like rotten leaves on the cold ground.

"I promise."

Only News. Never Opinions.   16 May

Dayton Valley News

Your Best Source of News Since 1965

Everly James, local South High junior has received a scholarship to attend Rutherford Academy for the 2020 school year. Ms. James was in a car accident a year ago with fellow student Caiden Jackson. James received devastating injuries and spent most of her sophomore year rehabilitating from her injuries. "Everly James' story is inspirational to us all," Darlene Hammond, Principal of South High, told reporters. Ms. James plans on majoring in English and told us, "she is very excited for this opportunity." Story Cont. A3.

Teen Receives Prestigious Scholarship After Tragic Accident.

17

THEN

I was awake, stuck in that blissful place between consciousness and deep sleep, still coming down from the high of what we'd just done. Jackson slept peacefully next to me, his face buried in the crook of my neck. I savored the feel of his breath against my skin.

Perfection. Even with Jackson's foreboding words before he fell asleep.

A buzzing noise grabbed my attention. It took me a second to realize that it was my phone. I carefully extricated myself from Jackson so that I could grab it from my jeans pocket.

It was Caiden.

We need to talk.

I felt sick reading the message. Especially considering the fact that not a day after breaking up with him, I had slept with his brother.

Despite the little voice inside of me that said it was better that I wait a few days for everyone's emotions to calm down, I decided to text him back. I loved Caiden, after all. Just not the way he wanted. There had to be a way that we could all move on from this. Caiden had always known that I loved Jackson. If I could just explain it to him, he had to understand.

Where do you want to meet?

His response was instant. *I'll pick you up.*

Panicking, I quickly told him to meet me in twenty minutes outside of my house, and I raced to quietly get dressed, figuring that I would be back before Jackson woke up.

I was five minutes late getting back to my house because the rain was so intense. After parking my bike in the driveway, I hurried to Caiden's Jeep.

"Hi," I said breathlessly as I got into the car and slammed the door. I was soaking wet once again.

I immediately started second-guessing my decision to meet him as soon as I saw Caiden.

His eyes looked even darker than usual, haunted. His skin looked ghastly under the dim lighting in the Jeep and his usually perfect hair was a mess.

"Caiden," I sighed softly, hating this situation, hating myself for what I had done, hating everything about this moment.

"Let's go for a drive," he said, taking off before I could respond.

I quickly put on my seatbelt and tried to be patient, even though I was itching to get away from him as my unease grew.

He was going a little too fast for my liking. Especially because the rain seemed to be getting even worse.

"Slow down," I yelped when we took a turn so fast that the tires slid out for a moment.

"You fucked him, didn't you?" he seethed in a voice so broken, it made my stomach clench.

"Caiden," I began.

"*Answer me*," he roared, pressing on the gas more.

"Please slow down," I answered as I began to sob, both from fear of the situation and sorrow for him and what I had done.

Not taking his eyes off the road, he grabbed my hair with one of his hands. I yelped and tried to move away from him, begging him to let go and stop.

"Do you know how much I fucking love you? I'm not letting you do this to us," he screamed, shaking my head viciously with his hold on my hair.

All I could do was cry. He was driving much too fast for me to try and jump out of the car, and his grip on my head was too strong for me to get away anyway.

I gave a small, hiccupped sigh of relief when he let go of my hair finally, but it was short lived. He backhanded me across the face and blood spurted onto the console in front of me.

He made a sound like a wounded animal. "You made me do this. This is your fault. You knew I wouldn't let you break up with me. You knew it." He continued to rage at me, his threats growing wilder and louder, punctuated by bashes to my face and the side of my head.

It was hard to think. I was close to losing consciousness, and I wasn't sure that I would survive tonight if I stayed in this car any longer.

Taking a chance, I slid my hand to the door handle. Caiden was still screaming, out of his mind, and wasn't watching me. Taking a deep breath to try and recover from the backhand I'd just taken to my cheekbone, I threw open the door.

Caiden swerved as I tried to unbuckle my seatbelt and

jump out. He cursed as he grabbed my shirt, trying to keep the Jeep on the road.

I managed to get my seatbelt undone, but Caiden was holding on to my shirt too tightly for me to be able to get away. I tried to beat at his hand, but he had managed to stop the Jeep, and his full attention was on me.

"You bitch," he screamed, and then everything went black as his fist crashed into my face one last time.

I WOKE up so out of it that it took me a second to figure out where I was and to remember what happened.

My door was closed again, and we were parked. Caiden was in the seat next to me, rocking back and forth and muttering to himself while smoking a cigarette.

I didn't even know that he smoked.

I failed to stifle my groan when the full force of my headache sprang to my attention. I shakily lifted a hand to my face and flinched when it was wet. Pulling my hand back, I grimaced. Blood covered it. He'd made a mess of me.

Caiden finally realized that I was awake. He reached out a hand towards me, his face written with regret. "I'm so fucking sorry, Everly—"

"Get away from me," I cried as I tried to move beyond his reach, not able to be touched by him.

What had I done to this beautiful boy? Had he always been like this, and I somehow had missed it? Or had I broken his heart so badly that all that was left inside of him was pain and ruin? As much as the outside of my body hurt, my heart hurt even worse.

There was no coming back from this. There was no way that I could stay in this town, stay by Caiden. There was no future for Jackson and me. Jackson would never forgive me for this. I would never forgive me for this.

Caiden suddenly pulled his hand away from me, a look of calm settling over his face that was somehow even more terrifying than his anger had been. What was he going to do? How could I get away from him?

He rubbed a hand over his eyes and then pushed his wet hair out of his face. He must have gotten out of the Jeep while I was unconscious. "I can fix this. It's going to be alright," he mumbled to himself. He clearly had lost his mind if he thought we could ever come back from this.

He had locked the doors, so there was no way that I could try and open the door again. So I was stuck when he began to drive. At least this time, he was going slower since the storm was still raging around us.

My phone began to buzz in my jeans. It had to be Jackson. I didn't really talk to anyone else besides the two of them. He must have woken up and seen that I was gone.

The sound caught Caiden's attention, and a dark look crossed his face. "Give me that," he ordered in a cool, deadly voice that sent chills spiraling across my body.

My hands shook as I fished the phone out of my pocket. There was a second where I debated answering it and begging for help. As the look on his face grew even more menacing, I foolishly decided to go for it, desperate to survive this night.

"Jackson," I cried out the second I hit the answer button. But Caiden was too quick. He ripped the phone out of my hand and opened his window, throwing my phone out into the storm.

"*No*," I cried out.

"You think you can get away from me? You think Jackson is going to save you? Jackson doesn't love you like I do. It's impossible for him to. You're not leaving this car until you forgive me or we're both dead," he spit at me.

I began to sob again. "This isn't you, Caiden. It's not you," I told him.

"I have no other choice, LyLy. I've loved you since the day I met you. I can't exist without you. And you keep pushing me. You keep acting like it doesn't matter. And I can't let you do that. I can't breathe without you," he said in a choked voice.

I buried my face into my hands, wincing at how bad it hurt.

"Just tell me you love me. Tell me you'll stay. I can forgive you for what happened with Jackson tonight. I can forgive you for anything but leaving me. Just say it," he begged me, beginning to speed up again as his emotions ramped up.

All of a sudden, the siren of a cop car started up behind us. A cop had obviously noticed that Caiden was driving close to ninety miles an hour on a forty miles per hour road.

I breathed a sigh of relief. This nightmare was about to be over.

But Caiden didn't stop. Instead, he started to push the Jeep even faster, and we were slipping all over the road as we raced along.

"Caiden, STOP," I screeched. I looked back and saw that the cop was trying to keep up but was having a hard time in these conditions against Caiden's suped-up engine.

"It's just going to be you and me, baby," he told me as he glanced at me, a wild look in his eyes and a wicked smile on his face. "Forever and ever," he said in a sing-song voice.

Suddenly, we slipped off the road, and this time, Caiden couldn't right the vehicle. It was as if time stood still as the car began to flip. Pieces of glass exploded on to us from the windshield, embedding into my skin as the car hit the ground before rolling again. My head smacked against the side of the car from the force of our movements and the airbags deployed as we continued to roll. Everything started to spin as we flipped a few more times before finally hitting some kind of pole and coming to a stop.

Blood was pouring down my face, and I was in so much pain that I couldn't move to look at Caiden. Smoke was coming through the broken windows.

I tried to cough, but my lungs made a funny gurgling sound when I attempted it. My chin fell forward as the muscles in my neck gave out, and I saw a jagged piece of glass sticking out from the middle of my chest.

I was dying. I had to be.

"No, no, no," came a cry from beside me, and my eyes closed briefly in relief that Caiden was still alive.

"I'll get us out of here. It's all going to be okay," he chanted as he moved next to me and tried to unbuckle my seatbelt.

"Stay with me," he begged, but I didn't even have the strength to look at him, let alone respond.

Everything started to fade from view, and all I could think was that I deserved this.

18

NOW

Jackson

Her beautiful eyes looked at me like I'd torn her world in two.

It occurred to me that my heart was still beating and I took breaths regularly as if on cue. But I wasn't sure how this was all working. I didn't feel anything. It was like my whole body had gone numb, and in my head, a refrain beat away.

Everly. Everly.

I'd lost her. There would be no coming back from today, this I knew. Everly and I were over, in a way so complete, it was almost as if we never existed together in the first place. The damage I had inflicted was so extensive, it sickened me, yet there was an underlying relief.

At last, I had finally gotten what I deserved—pain, rejection, self-loathing so intense that I couldn't imagine ever looking at myself in a mirror again—all of it washed over me, cleansing me, scouring me until I was raw and bloody and punished as I should have been the instant it all happened. These thoughts skittered through my mind, like pieces of glass in a shattered mirror.

The black was closing in now. I'd fought it until I was almost to my house. As soon as I crossed the threshold into my room, I gave in and felt my body being swept into the dark. I was alone here, and no one could save me in this place. The demons could come calling, and for now, they would win. All I could see was darkness. I was everything and I was nothing at the same time. I was a natural disaster and a ravaging force, yet somehow, I could not apologize.

She was gone.

It was my last thought for a very long while.

I wasn't sure if it'd been weeks or days as I slowly came out of what probably amounted to the worst depressive episode I'd ever experienced in my days since being diagnosed bipolar. My roommates had contemplated calling for an ambulance, but they must have changed their minds, since I was still laying here in my bed, surrounded by trash and dirty clothes. I hadn't showered in who knew how long, and the stink wafting from my body made my eyes water.

Shower. I should do that. Sooner rather than later.

Moving stiffly, I got up from my bed, looking around for my phone so I could find out what fucking day it actually was. It was dead of course. That was what happened when you lose all interest in life and everything that went with it.

I plugged it in. After a minute, it powered on and I saw that I had over twenty missed calls from my parents.

My heart was in my throat as I frantically pressed their number to call them back.

"Jackson?" My mom picked up on the first ring. She sounded...happy.

"Mom, is everything alright?" I asked in a voice hoarse from disuse.

"Baby, the most wonderful thing has happened..."

My mom never called me *baby*.

"What is it? You're freaking me out."

She took a trembling breath, and then uttered words that I never imagined I would ever hear.

"Caiden's awake."

Broken Hearts Academy is a duet and will conclude in *Heartbreak Lover*.

Get your copy here.

AUTHOR'S NOTE

This book was a labor of love. I got the idea about six months ago and started to work on it. And I worked...and I worked...and I worked. The words came easy, but other projects kept distracting me and it was really important to me that this book be exactly what I wanted. And I think I've managed just that. The good news is this book is a duet, so you won't have to deal with anymore cliffhangers. And hopefully I can redeem a few characters before we get to the end.

A few thank yous to my people. A big thanks to Heather Long for helping me get this book where I wanted it. Heather helped me add so much depth and kept me in line when I started to go off track. She had to edit it in chunks, but she never lost what my end goal was. Another thanks to Meghan from Bookish Dreams Editing for always being willing to edit my books on my crazy deadlines. It seriously takes a team.

Thanks to my ladies Rebecca Royce, Mila Young, and Raven Kennedy for pushing me to get the book done and encouraging me when I felt like I couldn't! Another thanks to my beta reader Caitlin M. for always loving my books. I'm a lucky girl to have so much support.

Thank you, my lovely readers, for sticking with me, sending me emails and messages of support, and generally being the very best people ever. I promise to torture you with dramatic cliffhangers for a very long time.

Keep Reading for a Look at Remember Us This Way, Book 1 of the completed Sound of Us Series

COPYRIGHT

Remember Us This Way by C. R. Jane
Copyright © 2019 by C. R. Jane

All rights reserved.

No portion of this book may be reproduced in any form or by any electronic or mechanical means, including information storage and retrieval systems, without written permission from the author, except for the use of brief quotations in a book review, and except as permitted by U.S. copyright law.

For permissions contact:

crjaneauthor@gmail.com

This book is a work of fiction. Names, characters, businesses, places, events, locales, and incidents are either the products of the author's imagination or used in a fictitious

Copyright

manner. Any resemblance to actual persons, living or dead, or actual events is purely coincidental.

REMEMBER US THIS WAY

They are idols to millions worldwide. I hear their names whispered in the hallways and blasted through the radio. Their faces are never far from the television screen, tormenting me with images of what I gave up.

To everyone else, they're unattainable rockstars, the music gods who make up The Sound of Us. But to me? They'll always be the boys I lost.

I broke all our hearts when I refused to follow them to L.A., convinced I would only bring them down. Years later, after I've succumbed to a monster, and my life has become something out of a nightmare, they are back.

I'm no longer the girl they left behind. But what if I've become the woman they can't forget?

PROLOGUE
BEFORE

According to the Sounds of Us Wikipedia page, the band hit almost instant stardom as soon as they finished recording their first album. A small indie band that had gained only regional notoriety, Red Label had taken a huge risk by signing them. The good looks and the killer voices of the three band members combined with the chance at a larger platform ended up making Sounds of Us the Label's most successful band in history. They released their first album, Death by Heartbreak, in 2013, and the first single, Follow You Into the Dark, made it to the Billboard Top 100 immediately.

It was their second single that propelled Sounds of Us to legend status though. Cold Heart was number one on the charts almost the second it was released. That led to four other songs ending up in the top ten. Three of them reached number one, with a fourth hitting number two on the charts. That album was torture in its finest form for me. Partly because I had lost them, but also partly because every one of those songs was about me. And that was just the hits. There were a lot more references in the songs that never got released as singles. It was a sharp stab in the chest to hear songs blaring from radios – songs whose lyrics contained exact words each of them had said to me, and that I had said to them.

And while some of the songs were wistful and pained, others were angry. Pissed-off. Occasionally enraged. It was uncomfortable. Actually, it was excruciating. At least for the first couple of months. I stopped listening to music eventually, something that had meant the world to me my entire life. I just couldn't handle the reminder of them anymore. My heart couldn't take it.

But every so often, a car would go by with its window down, or I'd walk past a motel room playing the radio, and I'd hear one of their voices and it would be an unexpected jolt of pain all over again.

After the release of their album, the band embarked on a short European tour, then followed it up with a much larger American tour. They started selling out stadiums. They appeared on every late-night show there was. Everyone wanted a piece of them. They were like this generation's Beatles, probably even bigger. The next two albums certainly were bigger, although those were easier for me to listen to since the songs about me faded as time went on. They were the most celebrated band in the world and there was no sign of their success slowing down anytime soon. It was everything they had ever dreamed about and that I had dreamed about with them.

They lived up to the bad boy image their label wanted to sell. Rumors of drug use and rampant women kept the gossip sites busy. I tried to ignore the magazines in the store racks by the checkout stand, but some of the pictures of the guys stumbling out of clubs with five girls each were a little too damning to be completely unfounded. And of course, there were the rumors that Tanner had secretly been in and out of rehab for the last two years in between tours. Tanner had always struggled with addiction but had only dabbled in hard drugs when I knew him. It wasn't hard for me to picture him struggling with them now that he probably had easy access to whatever he wanted from people desperate to please them all.

I often wondered if any part of the boys I knew were still around after I let myself give into my own addiction of catching up on any Sounds of Us news I could find. And then I would hear about them buying a house for someone who had lost everything in a natural disaster or hear of them participating in a charity drive to keep a no-kill shelter up and running, and I would know that a part of them was still there.

I've never made peace with letting them go. I never will.

CHAPTER 1
NOW

I hear the song come on from the living room. I had forgotten I had read that they were performing for New Year's Eve tonight in New York City before they embarked on their North American tour for the rest of the year. I wanted to avoid the room the music was coming from, but not even my hate for its current occupant could keep my feet from wandering to where the song was playing.

As I took that first step into the living room, and I saw Tanner's face up close, my heart clenched. As usual, he was singing to the audience like he was making love to them. When the camera panned to the audience, girls were literally fainting in the first few rows if he so much as ran his eyes in their direction. He swept a lock of his black hair out of his face, and the girls screamed even louder. Tanner had always had the bad boy look down perfectly. Piercing silver eyes that demanded sex, and full pouty lips you couldn't help but fantasize over, he was every mother's worst nightmare and every girl's naughty dream. I devoured his image like I was a crack addict desperate for one more hit. Usually

I avoided them like the plague, but junkies always gave in eventually. I was not the exception.

"See something you like?" comes a cold, amused voice that never ceases to fill me with dread. I curse my weakness at allowing myself to even come in the room. I know better than this.

"Just coming to see if you need a refill of your beer," I tell him nonchalantly, praying that he'll believe me, but knowing he won't.

My husband is sitting in his favorite armchair. He's a good-looking man according to the world's standards. Even I have to admit that despite the fact that the ugliness that lies inside his heart has long prevented me from finding him appealing in any way. His blonde hair is parted to the side perfectly, not a hair out of place. Sometimes I get the urge to mess it up, just so there can be an outward expression of the chaos that hides beneath his skin.

After I let the guys go, there was nothing left for me in the world. Instead of rising above my circumstances and becoming someone they would have been proud of, I became nothing. Gentry made perfectly clear that anything I was now was because of him.

Echoes of my lost heart beat inside my mind as another song starts to play on the television. It's the song that I know they wrote for me. It's angry and filled with betrayal, the kind of pain you don't come back from. The kind of pain you don't forgive.

Too late I realize that Gentry just asked me something and that my silence will tell him that I'm not paying attention to him. The sharp strike of his palm against my face sends me flying to the ground. I press my hand to my cheek as if I can stop the pain that is coursing through me. I already know this one will bruise. I'll have to wear an extra layer of makeup to cover it up when Gentry forces me to meet him at the country club tomorrow. After all, we wouldn't want anyone at the club to know that our lives are anything less than perfect.

The song is still going and somehow the pain I hear in Tanner's voice hurts me more than the pain blossoming across my cheek. Would it not hurt them as much if they knew everything I had told them to sever our connection permanently was a lie? Would they even care at this point that I had done it to set them free, to stop them from being dragged down into the hell I never seemed to be able to escape from? At night, when I lay in bed, listening to the sound of Gentry sleeping peacefully as if the world was perfect and monsters didn't exist, I told myself that it would matter.

"Get up," snaps Gentry, yanking me up from the floor. I'm really off my game tonight by lingering. Nothing makes Gentry madder than when I "wallow" as he calls it. As I stumble out of the room, my head spinning a bit from the force of the hit, a sick part of me thinks it was worth it, just so I could hear the end of their song.

※

LATER THAT NIGHT, long after I should have fallen asleep, my mind plays back what little of the performance I saw earlier. I wonder if Jensen still gets severe stage fright before he performs. I wonder if Jesse still keeps his lucky guitar pick in his pocket during performances. I wonder who Tanner gets his good luck kiss from now.

It all hurts too much to contemplate for too long so I grab the Ambien I keep on my bedside table for when I can't sleep, which is often, and I drift off into a dreamland filled with a silver eyed boy who speaks straight to my soul.

The next morning comes too early and I struggle to wake up when Gentry's alarm goes off. Ambien always leaves me groggy and I haven't decided what's better, being exhausted from not sleeping, or taking half the day to wake up all the way.

Throwing a robe on, I blurrily walk to the kitchen to get Gentry's protein shake ready for him to take with him to the gym.

I'm standing in front of the blender when Gentry comes up behind me and puts his arms around me, as if the night before never happened. I'm very still, not wanting to make any sudden movement just in case he takes it the wrong way.

"Meet me at the club for lunch," he asks, running his nose up the side of my neck and eliciting shivers...the wrong kind of shivers. He's using his charming voice, the one that always gets everyone to do what he wants. It stopped working on me a long time ago.

"Of course," I tell him, turning in his arms and giving him a wide, fake smile. What else would my answer be when I know the consequences of going against Gentry's wishes?

"Good," he says with satisfaction, placing a quick, sharp kiss on my lips before stepping away.

I pour the blended protein shake into a cup and hand it to him. "11:45?" I ask. He nods and waves goodbye as he walks out of the house to head to the country club gym where he'll spend the next several hours working out with his friends, flirting with the girls that work out there, and overall acting like the overwhelming douche that he is.

I don't relax until the sound of the car fades into the

distance. After eating a protein shake myself (Gentry doesn't approve of me eating carbs), I start my chores for the day before I have to get ready to meet him at the country club.

My hands are red and raw from washing the dishes twice. Everything was always twice. Twice bought me time and ensured there wouldn't be anything left behind. An errant fleck of food, a spot that hadn't been rinsed – these were things he'd notice.

Hours later, I've vacuumed, swept, done the laundry, and cleaned all the bathrooms. Gentry could easily afford a maid, but he likes me to "keep busy" as he puts it, so I do everything in this house of horrors. I repeat the same things every day even though the house is in perfect condition. I would clean every second if it meant that he was out of the house permanently though.

I straighten the pearls around my neck and think for the thousandth time that if I ever escape this hell hole, I'm going to burn every pearl I come across. I'm dressed in a fitted pastel pink dress that comes complete with a belt ordained with daisies. Five years ago, I wouldn't have been caught dead in such an outfit but far be it for me to wear jeans to a country club. I slip into a pair of matching pastel wedges and then run out to the car. I'm running late and I can only hope that he's distracted and doesn't realize the time.

As I drive, I can't help but daydream. Dream about what it would have been like if I had joined the guys in L.A. Bellmont is a sleepy town that's been the same for generations. I haven't been anywhere outside of the town since I got married except to Myrtle Beach for my honeymoon.

The town is steeped in history, a history that it's very proud of. The main street is still perfectly maintained from the early 1900s, and I've always loved the whitewashed look of the buildings and the wooden shingles on every roof. The town attracts a vast array of tourists who come here to be close to the beach. They can get a taste of the coastal southern flavor of places like Charleston and Charlotte, but they don't have to pay as high of a price tag.

It's a beautiful prison to me, and if I ever manage to escape from it, I never want to see it again.

I turn down a street and start down the long drive that leads to Bellmont's most exclusive country club. The entire length of the road is sheltered by large oak trees and it never ceases to make me feel like an extra in Gone With the Wind whenever I come here. The feeling is only reinforced when I pull up to the large, freshly painted white plantation house that's been converted into the club.

My blood pressure spikes as I near the valet stand. Just knowing that I'm about to see Gentry and all of his friends is enough to send my pulse racing. I smile nervously at the teenage boy who is manning the stand and hand him my keys. He gives me a big smile and a wink. It reminds me of something that Jesse used to do to older women to make them swoon, and my heart clenches. Is there ever going to be a day when something doesn't remind me of one of them?

I ignore the valet boy's smile and walk inside, heading to the bar where I can usually find Gentry around lunch time. I pause as I walk inside the lounge. Wendy Perkinson is leaning against Gentry, pressing her breasts against him, much too close for propriety's sake. I know I should probably care at least a little bit, but the idea of Gentry turning his attentions away from me and on to Wendy permanently is more than I can even wish for. I'm sure he's fucked her, the way she's practically salivating over him as he talks to his friend blares it loudly, but unfortunately that's all she will ever get from him. Gentry's obsession with me has thus far proved to be a lasting thing. But since I finally started refusing to sleep with him after the beatings became a regular thing, he goes elsewhere for his so-called needs when he doesn't feel like trying to force me. At least a few times a week I'm assaulted by the stench of another woman's perfume on my husband's clothes. It's become just another unspoken thing in my marriage.

Martin, Gentry's best friend, is the first to see me and his eyes widen when he does. He coughs nervously, the poor thing thinking I actually care about the situation I've walked into. Gentry looks at him and then looks at the entrance where he sees me standing there. His eyes don't widen in anything remotely resembling remorse or shame...we're too far past that at this point. He does extricate himself from Wendy's grip however to start walking towards me, his gaze devouring me as he does so. One thing I've never doubted in my relationship with Gentry is how beautiful he thinks I am.

"You're gorgeous," he tells me, kissing me on the cheek and putting a little too much pressure on my arm as he guides me to the bar. Wendy has moved farther down the bar, setting her sights on another married member of the club. It's funny to me that in high school I had wanted to stab her viciously when she set her sights on Jesse, but when she actually sleeps with my husband I could care less.

"My parents are waiting in the dining hall. You're ten minutes late," says Gentry, again squeezing my arm to emphasize his displeasure with me. I sigh, pasting the fake smile on my face that I know he expects. "There was traffic," I say simply, and I let him lead me to the dining hall where the second worst thing about Gentry is waiting for us.

Gentry's mother, Lucinda, considers herself southern

royalty. Her parents owned the largest plantation in South Carolina and spoiled their only daughter with everything that her heart desired. This of course made her perhaps the most self-obsessed woman I had ever met, and that was putting it lightly. Gentry's father, Conrad, stands as we approach, dressed up in the suit and tie that he wears everywhere regardless of the occasion. Like his son, Gentry's father was a handsome man. Although his hair was slightly greying at the temples, his face remained impressively unlined, perhaps due to the same miracle worker that made his wife look forever thirty-five.

"Darling, you look wonderful as always," he tells me, brushing a kiss against my cheek and making we want to douse myself in boiling water. Conrad had no qualms about propositioning his son's wife. I couldn't remember an interaction I'd had with him that hadn't ended with him asking me to sneak away to the nearest dark corner with him. I purposely choose to sit on the other side of Gentry, next to his mother, although that option isn't much better. She looks me over, pursing her lips when she gets to my hair. According to her, a proper southern lady keeps her hair pulled back. But I've never been a proper lady, and the guys always loved my hair. Keeping it down is my silent tribute to them and the person I used to be since everything else about me is almost unrecognizable.

Lucinda is a beautiful woman. She's always impeccably dressed, and her mahogany hair is always impeccably coiffed. She's also as shallow as a teacup. She begins to chatter, telling me all about the town gossip; who's sleeping with who, who just got fake boobs, whose husband just filed for bankruptcy. It all passes in one ear and out the other until I hear her say something that sounds unmistakably like "Sounds of Us."

I look up at her, catching her off guard with my sudden interest. "Sorry, could you repeat that?" I ask. Her eyes are gleaming with excitement as she clasps her hands delicately in front of herself. She waits to speak until the waiter has refilled her glass with water. She slowly takes a sip, drawing out the wait now that she actually has my attention.

"I was talking about the Sounds of Us concert next week. They are performing two shows. Everyone's going crazy over the fact that the boys will be coming home for the first time since they made it big. It's been what...four years?" she says.

"Five," I correct her automatically, before cursing myself when she smirks at me.

"So, you aren't immune to the boys' charms either..." she says with a grin.

"What was that, Mother?" asks Gentry, his interest of course rising at the mention of anything to do with me and other men.

"I was just telling Ariana about the concert coming to town," she says. I hold my breath waiting to hear if she will mention the name. Gentry's so clueless about anything that doesn't involve him that he probably hasn't heard yet that they're coming to town.

"Ariana doesn't like concerts," he says automatically. It's his go-to excuse for making sure I never attend any social functions that don't involve him. Ariana doesn't like sushi. Ariana doesn't like movies. The list of times he's said such a thing go on and on. I feel a slight pang in my chest. Ariana. Gentry and his family insist on calling me by my full name, and I miss the days where I had relationships that were free and easy enough to use my nickname of Ari.

"Of course she doesn't, dear," says Lucinda, patting my hand. The state of my marriage provides much amusement to Lucinda and Conrad. Both approve of the Gentry's "heavy hand" towards me and although they haven't witnessed the abuse first hand, they're well aware of Gentry's penchant for using me as a punching bag. Gentry's parents are simply charming.

I pick at my salad and listen to Lucinda prattle on, my interest gone now that she's off the subject of the concert. Gentry and his dad are whispering back and forth, and I can feel Gentry shooting furtive glances at me. I know I should be concerned or at least interested about what their talking about, but my mind has taken off, thinking about the fact that in just a few days' time, the guys will be in the same vicinity as me for the first time in five years. If only....

"Ariana," says Gentry, pulling me from my day dream. I immediately pull on the smile I have programmed to flash whenever I'm in public with Gentry.

"Yes?"

"I think you've had enough to eat," he tells me as if he's talking about the weather and not the fact that he's just embarrassed me in front of everyone at the table.

I shakily set my fork down, my cheeks flushing from his comment. I was eating a salad and I'm already slimmer than I should be. But Gentry loves to control everything about me, food being just one of many things. I see Lucinda patting her lips delicately as she finishes eating her salmon. My stomach growls at the fact that I've had just a few bites to eat. I have a few dollars stashed away in my car, I'll have to stop somewhere and grab something to eat on the way home. That is if Gentry doesn't leave at the same time as me and follow me.

When I've gotten my emotions under control, I finally lift my eyes and glance at my husband. He's back in deep conversation with Conrad, their voices still too soft for me to pick anything up. Looking at him, I can't help but get the urge to stab him with my silverware and then run screaming from the room. The bastard would probably find a way to haunt me from the grave even if he didn't survive. Still, I find my hand clenching involuntarily as if grasping for a phantom knife.

After that one terrible night when it became clear that I couldn't go to L.A. to meet up with the guys, I was lost. I got a job as a waitress and was living in one of those pay by week extended stay motels since there was no way I could stay in my trailer with *them* anymore. I met Gentry Mayfield while waitressing one night. He was handsome and charming, and persevered in asking me out even when I refused the first half a dozen times. My heart was broken, how could I even think of trying to give my broken self to someone else? I finally got tired of saying no and went on a date with him. He made me smile, something that I didn't think was possible, and every date after that seemed to be more perfect than I deserved. I didn't fall in love with Gentry, my heart belonged to three other men, but I did develop admiration and fondness for Gentry in a way that I hadn't thought possible. After pictures started to surface on the first page of the gossip sites of the guys with hordes of beautiful women, and the fact that my life seemed to be going nowhere, marrying Gentry seemed to be the second chance that I didn't deserve. Except the funny thing about how it all turned out is that my life with Gentry turned out worse than I probably deserved, even after everything that had happened.

Three months after we were married, I burnt dinner. Gentry had come home in a bad mood because of something that had happened at work. Apparently, me burning dinner was the last straw for him that day and he struck me across the face, sending me flying to the ground. Afterwards, he begged and pleaded with me for forgiveness, saying it would never happen again. But I wasn't stupid, I knew how this story played out. I stayed for a week so that I could get ahold of as much money as I could and then I drove off while he was at work. I was stopped at the state lines by a trooper who evidently was friends with Gentry's family. I was dragged kicking and screaming back home where Gentry was waiting, furious and ready to make me pay. Every semblance of the man that I had thought I was marrying was gone.

I had $5,000 to my name when I met him. I'd gotten it from selling the trailer that I inherited when my parents died in a car crash after one of their drunken nights out on the town. Gentry had convinced me that I should put it in our "joint account" right after we got married and stupidly, I had agreed to do it. I never got access to that account. Gentry stole my money, he stole my self-esteem. No, he didn't steal it, he chipped away at it and just when I thought I'd crumble, he kissed me and cried over me and told me he'd die without me.

I tried to get away several more times, by bus, on foot, I even went to the police to try and report him. But the Mayfield's had everyone in this state in their pocket, and nothing I said or did worked. I eventually stopped trying. It had taken me a year of not running away to get my car back and to be able to do things other than stay home, locked in our bedroom, while Gentry was at work.

Gentry stood up from the table, bringing me back to the present. A random song lyric floated through my mind about how the devil wears a pretty face, it certainly fit Gentry Mayfield.

"I'm heading to the office for the rest of the day. What

are your plans?" he asks, as if I had a choice in what my plans were.

"Just finishing things around the house and going to the store to get a few ingredients for dinner," I tell him, waving a falsely cheerful goodbye to Gentry's parents as he walks me out of the dining area towards the valet stand. We stop by the exit and he pulls me towards him, stroking the side of my face that I've painted with makeup to hide the bruise he gave me the night before. My eyes flutter from the rush of pain but Gentry somehow mistakes it as the good kind of reaction to his touch. He leans in for a kiss.

"You're still the most beautiful woman I've ever seen," he tells me, sealing his lips over mine in a way that both cuts off my air supply and makes me want to wretch all at once. I hold still, knowing that it will enrage him that I don't do anything in response to his kiss, but not having it in me to fake more than I already have for the day. He pulls back and searches my eyes for something, I'm not sure what. He must not find it because his own eyes darken, and his grip on my arms suddenly tightens to a point that wouldn't look like anything to a club passerby, but that will inevitably leave bruises on my too pale skin.

He leans in and brushes his lips against my ear. "You're never going to get away from me, so when are you going to just give in?" he spits out harshly. I say nothing, just stare at him stonily. I can see the storm building in his eyes.

"Don't bother with dinner, I'll be home late," he says, striding away without a second glance, probably to go find Wendy and make plans to fuck her after he leaves the office, or maybe it will be at the office knowing him.

I wearily make my way through the doors to the valet stand and patiently wait for my keys. It's a different kid this time and I'm grateful he doesn't try to flirt with me.

On my way back from the country club I find myself taking the long way back to the house, the way that takes me by the trailer park where I grew up. I park by the office trailer and find myself walking to the field behind the rows of homes. Looking at the trash riddled ground, I gingerly walk through the mud, flecks of it hitting the formerly pristine white fabric of my shoes. I walk until I get to an abandoned fire pit that doesn't look like it's been used for quite a while. For probably five years to be exact.

I sit on a turned over trash barrel until the sun sits precariously low in the sky and I know that I'm playing with fire if I dare to stay any longer. I then get up and walk back to my car, passing by the trailer I once lived in. It's funny that after everything that has happened, at the moment I would give anything to be back in that trailer again.

> Discover the rest of this **COMPLETED** series at
> books2read.com/rememberusthisway

JOIN C.R.'S FATED REALM

A Texas girl living in Utah now, I'm a wife, mother, lawyer, and now author. My stories have been floating around in my head for years, and it has been a relief to finally get them down on paper. I'm a huge Dallas Cowboys fan and I primarily listen to Beyonce and Taylor Swift...don't lie and say you don't too.

My love of reading started probably when I was three and with a faster than normal ability to read, I've devoured hundreds of thousands of books in my life. It only made sense that I would start to create my own worlds since I was always getting lost in others'. I like heroines who have to grow in order to become badasses, happy endings, and swoon-worthy, devoted, (and hot) male characters. If this sounds like you, I'm pretty sure we'll be friends. I'm so glad to have you on my team...check out the links below for ways to hang out with me and more of my books you can read!

Visit my **Facebook** page to get updates.
    Visit my **Amazon Author** page.

Join C.R.'s Fated Realm

Visit my **Website**.

Sign up for my **newsletter** to stay updated on new releases, find out random facts about me, and get access to different points of view from my characters.

OTHER BOOKS BY C.R. JANE

The Fated Wings Series
First Impressions

Forgotten Specters

The Fallen One (a Fated Wings Novella)

Forbidden Queens

Frightful Beginnings (a Fated Wings Short Story)

Faded Realms

Faithless Dreams

Fabled Kingdoms (2020)

The Rock God (a Fated Wings Novella)

The Timeless Affection Series
Lamented Pasts

Lost Passions

The Sounds of Us Contemporary Series (complete series)
Remember Us This Way

Remember You This Way

Remember Me This Way

Broken Hearts Academy Series
Heartbreak Prince

Heartbreak Lover

The Pack Queen Series

Queen of the Thieves

Queen of the Alphas (2020)

The Rise Again Series

The Day After Nothing (2020)

Academy of Souls Co-write with Mila Young (complete series)

School of Broken Souls

School of Broken Hearts

School of Broken Dreams

School of Broken Wings

Fallen World Series Co-write with Mila Young (complete series)

Bound

Broken

Betrayed

Belong

Thief of Hearts Co-write with Mila Young

Siren Condemned

Siren Sacrificed

Standalone Co-write with Mila Young

The Naughty List

Stupid Boys Series Co-write with Rebecca Royce

Stupid Boys

Dumb Girl

Crazy Love

Printed in Dunstable, United Kingdom